Scars of Salem:

K'wan Presents

URBAN FICTION

MAR   2017

JF

Scars of Salem:

K'wan Presents

Niles Manning

www.urbanbooks.net

Urban Books, LLC
97 N18th Street
Wyandanch, NY 11798

Scars of Salem: K'wan Presents
Copyright © 2016 Niles Manning

ISBN 13: 978-1-62286-729-5
ISBN 10: 1-62286-729-7

First Mass Market Printing November 2016
Printed in the United States of America

10 9 8 7 6 5 4 3 2 1

This is a work of fiction. Any references or similarities to actual events, real people, living or dead, or to real locales are intended to give the novel a sense of reality. Any similarity in other names, characters, places, and incidents is entirely coincidental.

Distributed by Kensington Publishing Corp.
Submit Orders to:
Customer Service
400 Hahn Road
Westminster, MD 21157-4627
Phone: 1-800-733-3000
Fax: 1-800-659-2436

Scars of Salem:

K'wan Presents

by

Niles Manning

Prologue

The five kids made their way down the dead-end street as lively chatter circulated among them. One kid was quiet, though, and the loud voices made him nervous as he kept looking around his familiar surroundings. Dontarious slowed his stride as the group moved on in front of him. He glanced to his right and saw the last house on the block, and a chill pulsated through his nervous system. An old friend lived there. They were previously best friends in their childhood days, but now that they were headed into their sophomore year of high school, they had gone their separate ways.

While Dontarious had matured and found more importance in things different than the childish games of junior high, his friend stayed the same. Every now and then, Dontarious would see him around the neighborhood. He would speak, even chill with him for a bit, but eventually he'd break away to rejoin his new group of friends. It was a sad case, but Dontarious's childhood friend just never grew up into the personality that high school demanded. Dontarious was now into chasing girls, dressing in name brand clothing, and planning for college. His friend was still doing the same shit they did in their adolescence: running through the woods playing war games, torturing animals, petty theft, and any form of immature mischief. Dontarious felt as if he had advanced from such.

"Man, let's go in the woods and fuck some shit up!" Brandon said excitedly.

Dontarious shook his head as he sped up to rejoin them. Brandon led the pack and turned to them as he chambered a round into the varmint rifle he was carrying. He was the self-proclaimed leader, only because his parents had money and didn't mind dishing it out. He was a spoiled nuisance, but the girls loved him, and he didn't mind sharing his spoils with his loyal followers.

"What? Y'all looking at me like y'all scared or some shit," Brandon analyzed the group. The other four members turned their heads between each other, gauging if anyone else had a better idea. Not a soul spoke up.

It was the last day of the summer break, so Brandon wanted to create one last memory of havoc before the school year started. "Nigga, you talking about going in those woods? You got me fucked up," Jontai spoke up.

He was a tall, dark-skinned soul with dusty cornrows that stopped at his ears. Out of the bunch, he was the gangster, the hoodlum, and the brute who blinked red eyes of trouble, and that's essentially why Brandon kept him around—to watch his ass.

"You think we're about to walk in those woods? Man, you tripping this time, Bran," Quinten spoke. He was the runt of the group, soft-spoken, and often teased as the scaredy-cat.

Brandon ignored his comment and shook his head before he looked at Jontai again. Dontarious was in the back of the group, keeping an eye on his old friend's house, praying that he didn't come outside and embarrass himself. His new group of friends would show no mercy in their taunts, and knowing his friend, he wouldn't take the hint until it was far too late.

"Nigga, we have this," Brandon said as he held the rifle up like a field lieutenant briefing an upcoming charge. "So why are y'all acting like bitches—pussyfooting and shit?"

"Fool, that weak-ass gun couldn't kill a rabbit!" Scott said from off to the side. He was a pretty boy, and his demeanor screamed it. His clothing stayed fresh, as well as his oily curls on top of his fade, inherited by his Spanish mother. "The fuck we gon' do if we see a bear or some shit? And don't think I'm about to walk through that bullshit in these kicks!" he said as he lifted one foot, showing off his new Butta Tims.

Dontarious glanced back at the house. He thought he heard something.

"Ain't no bears in these woods, right?" Quinten tried to convince himself. His eyes bounced among them looking for an answer. His continued paranoia was frequently ignored by the other members.

"What else we gon' do then? Man, stop bitching out on me. I just want to see what that so-called haunted house looks like that I hear is back there," Brandon said as he slouched in disappointment. He was an amateur at the technique, but he was slowly honing his manipulative skills.

"Haunted house?" Quinten mumbled. His big eyes on his small round face seemed to bulge animatedly.

"It's not haunted. It's just old," Dontarious threw in.

He was hoping they didn't ask how he knew. He'd be forced to expose himself and his early escapades with his weird friend through those very woods. That was a gray chapter of his past that steadily tried to surface to light.

"Nigga, how you know?" Brandon asked.

"Man, fuck it! Y'all working my nerves out here with that bickering shit. Let's just get it over with," Jontai said as he marched forward.

Brandon dashed beside him with the rifle, while the rest of the group was hesitant, but eventually followed down the wooded path.

In a single file line, they marched down the narrow trail with Brandon at the lead. Jontai was right behind him with his hands tucked inside his hoodie. Scott followed him, stepping gingerly over mud puddles, careful not to scuff his shoes before school started. Every now and then, he'd complain and get silenced by Jontai. Behind Scott was Quinten. He treaded timidly with his head on a greased pivot, eying every noise that he heard in the environment. At the back of the line was Dontarious. He wasn't as tense as the others; he had traveled that path on many occasions, even at night, and could find his way out of the woods blindfolded; his worries were deeper than nature's threat.

"Gotdamn!" Scott shouted as he grabbed his leg. Everyone turned toward him to see what the ruckus was about. "Fucking mosquitoes and shit!" he said as he rubbed his reddened skin with a face of annoyance.

"Man, shut yo' diva ass up. I thought you got bit by a snake by the way you was screaming like a bitch," Jontai said as he turned and shoved Brandon to continue the trek.

"They got snakes out here?" Quinten asked while fanning a spiderweb from his face, but as usual, his question went unanswered. Nobody wanted to think about that, not even Dontarious—he had seen plenty of snakes out there.

Finally, after fifteen minutes of walking, Scott complaining, Quinten questioning, and Jontai cursing, their journey had reached its pinnacle. Brandon blindly pushed through a brush of branches and stepped out into a clear area of the woodland. The rest of the crew followed suit as they stood next to him and looked up at what he was staring at. Before them was a two-story home that looked as if it was a Hollywood prop for the opening scene to a horror flick. Weeds covered the front porch and wrapped around the house as if the earth was consuming the residence. The windows were boarded up as well as the door, probably to keep wildlife out—or something in.

The tin roof was rusted and matched the discolored moldering wood of the structure. The boys breathed easy, as it seemed that if one wrong move, deep breath, or a heavy blink occurred, the house would cave into the soil, causing a sinkhole.

"Yo, that shit look spooky as fuck," Jontai said as he took a careful step. The twigs broke beneath his shoe and echoed like bones being snapped in a wet basement.

"I told y'all. Y'all never wanna believe yo' boy," Brandon said. He was happy that they found it, and he didn't look crazy for leading them on yet another "Dummy Mission."

Dontarious stepped off to the side and stuffed his hands into the pockets of his jeans. He had seen the house a hundred times, but he had to play it like he was shocked as well. He did a lot to fit in with his new ensemble of friends, and sometimes he felt like the outcast that he was running from. The irony alone ironed out the wrinkles on his conscience and creased a guilty frown on his heart. He wasn't proud of the way he treated the old friend lately, but the new Dontarious needed to fit in—he need to fit or become exposed as a lame like his friend, once the hem was discovered and the truth rolled out.

"Who would live out here in a place like this?" Quinten asked.

He swatted a mosquito from his neck and pulled his collar up as a defense mechanism.

He didn't like the vibe he was getting from the house . . . or the area. They were deep in the woods, and if something was to happen to them, it would be hours, days, weeks, or probably forever before somebody found them—he was freaking himself out.

"Man, this piece of shit was built back in them slave days. Probably had a big, sweaty, ugly muthafucka like Jontai sitting on the porch chewing a broom straw," Scott joked. Jontai playfully swung at him as they circled around in horseplay. Dontarious had an epiphany. His new friends were no different.

"Y'all chill out," Brandon ordered.

He stepped to the side to get a better view of the house. He held the rifle forward like a soldier, or more like he had seen in the movies, as he inspected the exterior of the raddled home. He wanted to go inside—well, "he" didn't, but he wanted to know what was inside, and know what it looked like.

"This shit gotta be haunted, like on the real," he said as he faced his crew and started walking back toward them.

A voice from behind them made every present soul almost abandon their skin. "It's not haunted. It's just old." A figure emerged from the path with a hoodie pulled up tightly.

Dontarious recognized him immediately and dropped his head. The figure walked toward them and removed his hood like a ninja as he folded his scrawny arms across his skeletal chest.

"Look at this muthafucka here . . . Scaring the shit out of us! The fuck you doing out here, Salem?" Jontai asked.

Everyone knew Salem as the weirdo of the neighborhood. He was quiet, distanced, and a bum to the eyes of the in-crowd. His clothes were always dirty and ripped. His hoodie had served him faithfully for years, and its loyalty weakened in its threads. He was tall, taller than Jontai, but lanky. His face always looked ashy. He smelled of outdoor voyages and cheap deodorant. His shoes used to be white, but now they were beige with slime soles as if he had been mowing the lawn at a White House inauguration. His whole appearance was lame, goofy, and the kid in the back of the class that everyone looked over until it was time to tease somebody. That was Salem, a demeanor of chaos titled by a name that meant peace.

"How you know it isn't haunted?" Brandon asked as he walked up and joined the group.

Dontarious knew the scene was about to get hectic at the expense of his old friend's feelings, and there was nothing that he could do about it.

"He probably lives here. Look at his gear. Bum-ass nigga look like crackhead Pooky's 'Before & After' picture," Scott clowned. Laughter erupted among them as Dontarious shook his head and stared at the ground; he did that so much that his neck was starting to ache.

"That nigga be out here wrestling raccoons and shit. Look at his fucked-up-ass jeans. Look like he just stole third base!" Scott was on a roll, but Salem didn't seem fazed by the insults. He stepped forward and faced the house. "He probably a ghost his damn self. Nigga look dead. Nigga look like he died twice. Nigga look . . ." Scott couldn't contain his laughter. "Nigga look like he just walked off the set of *Thriller!* He was an extra and required no makeup! Who taught you how to dress? Flip from *Above the Rim?*"

Quinten felt bad for Salem. He used to be the butt of Scott's jokes, but they kept Quinten around for one purpose. For some reason, the girls found his small physique and baby face adorable. Now a new target had emerged, but Quinten knew what it felt like to be in the cross-hairs of a joking session . . . to have to stand there and take it, praying that they run out of material or move on to another victim.

"This old family used to live here back in the day. My grandma told me about them. Weird family," Salem said as he pointed at the house like a homeless realtor.

"Nigga, you got some nerve to call somebody weird," Jontai spoke.

He never liked Salem. He always wanted to punch a hole in his face, but he never secured a valid reason for his bullylike urge.

"Did they die in it?" Brandon asked as he held the rifle to his side. He was extremely curious.

"Nah. They just disappeared," Salem responded.

"How you know they didn't die in it?" Brandon threw back at him. He liked that theory better.

"My grandma told me."

"*My grandma told me, my grandma told me . . .*" Scott mocked Salem in a pesky voice. "Nigga, shut yo' lame ass up. Yo' grandma ain't told you shit! She don't even like yo' ass! You know you ain't shit when your grandma try to abort you."

"Go look," Brandon said as the laughter faded.

Everyone got quiet and looked as Salem turned to Brandon and frowned his face up.

"What you mean?" Salem asked.

"Go inside," Brandon lifted the rifle into both hands and nodded toward the house, "and look—"

"Hell no. Ain't no telling what's in there," Salem responded.

Brandon aimed the rifle at Salem as the crowd backed up. Dontarious opened his mouth, but words didn't come out. He knew this would happen but did nothing to stop it.

"You got two options. You can go inside like I told you, or I can shoot yo' dog ass right here." Brandon's eyes were cold as he looked down the sight of the weapon.

"You just gon' have to sho—" Salem started, but the loud pop of the rifle cracked the air.

He fell to a knee as he grabbed his leg. The shot had ripped a new hole in his jeans, and his leg felt like it was on fire and ice. Scott was hunched over dying in laughter. Jontai was smiling. He enjoyed seeing Salem in pain as he grunted and held his wound. Quinten was quiet, and Dontarious did nothing. As always—he just watched and shook his head as his new friends assaulted his old one.

"Chill, man!" Salem said as he held his palm forward with his free hand—he looked as if he was directing traffic, stalling an oncoming train wreck that was headed right for him.

It was his fault; he knew that they were loco, he heard the commotion, saw the steam, and still chose to stand on their tracks. He stood to his feet and almost buckled from the pain.

"You gon' go inside?" Brandon asked. The shot was actually an accident, but he played it off well.

"Nah, that's crazy! Just chill . . ." Salem pleaded. He appealed like the whimpers of a wounded animal, and that's exactly how they viewed him—like a varmint.

Brandon chambered another round in the rifle with a menace on his face. He was used to being in control, and having someone defy him pushed him to a new level of hatred.

"Muthafuckas don't believe shit stink till they smell it!" he said as he raised the rifled and took aim.

"A'ight, chill," Salem said as he slowly turned back toward the house but kept an eye on Brandon and the threat on his peripheral. "The windows and doors are blocked. How do you expect me to get inside?"

"You're a crafty little fuck. Find a way," Brandon said as he kept his aim.

Dontarious watched in silence. There was nothing he could do—or at least that's what he told himself. What did Salem think would happen when he showed up? He was always getting himself into these situations, and one would think he'd learned his lesson about trying to fit in . . . but who was Dontarious to judge?

Salem looked and saw a window on the second floor that wasn't boarded shut. That would be a perfect entrance; maybe not perfect, but it was the only choice that he had, unless he decided to just take off running. He turned and looked at Dontarious who dropped his head. That hurt more than the bullet wound . . .

"Go'n head up there," Brandon said as he noticed the window too. Salem limped through the weeds and touched the side of the house. It felt as if it would collapse at any second. He grabbed the top of the first-floor window and pulled himself up. Cautiously, he placed his foot on a piece of wood that was protruding and stepped higher.

"Nigga look like a broke-ass Spider-Man . . . Nah, his black ass look like venom."

Salem could hear the jokes still being fired at him as he climbed higher. When he finally reached the window, his heart sank at the sight of an old heavy dresser blocking the way. He balanced himself and tried to push it to the side, but it seemed as if it was nailed to the floor. He hung and looked down at Brandon.

"It's blocked."

Brandon sucked his teeth. "Find another way!" He was feeling himself now. The power gave him a rush as another human being followed his every command praying for mercy that he wouldn't hurt him. "Go to the roof."

"The *roof?* And do what?" Salem asked as he hung on like he was fixing a telephone line.

"Go through the chimney, nigga!" Jontai shouted.

Salem looked at Brandon.

"Go."

He reached up and grabbed whatever he could to pull himself up. Little by little he made his way to the top as Dontarious watched on with the rest of them. Salem knew that he wasn't going through a chimney, but he was hoping that he could find another way in to appease his new "friends."

As he pulled himself onto the roof, he could hear the tin groan beneath his weight. It seemed to bend and sink, but he stood to his feet and looked around. As suspected, there wasn't another entrance inside. He turned and looked over the edge at Brandon. "No way in."

"The chimney!" Brandon shouted back at him.

Salem had had enough. They would just have to shoot him, because there was no way he was going to slide down into a potential snake pit.

"Nah, fuck that!"

"What you say?" Brandon said as he stepped forward and aimed the rifle again.

"I said fuck that, and fuck you if you think I'm about to do that dumb shit."

It got quiet. Even the crickets that surrounded them stopped chirping like a dead two-way. The wind stopped blowing as Mother Nature held her breath. The sun turned down its contrast as a dark cloud filtered its rays. A slave had defied a god, and the earth's axis seemed to bend as the gravity of reality hit Brandon, reminding him of how powerless he really was.

"Damn, son, you gon' let him talk to you like that?" Scott instigated.

Brandon looked on, but he just couldn't do it. He wanted to pull the trigger, but once his power of influence was removed and his card was pulled, his true character was revealed as a small joker. He lowered the rifle and shook his head. Jontai snapped his attention toward him and read his face in disgust.

"Man, you a straight bitch!" Jontai said as he snatched the rifle and aimed it at Salem.

Salem just looked at him, and not a blotch of fear was displayed on his muted face. He even stuck his hands in his pockets and shrugged. He looked to the side and met Dontarious's eyes for the first time. He could see the guilt in his pupils as he stood among his peers and acted blind to their old friendship.

"There is only one way this can end, and I think you've read this book before," Jontai said as he smoothed his finger over the trigger.

"Go ahead, narrator, tell the people how it ends," Salem said as he spread his arms out, welcoming fate.

Jontai smiled. He finally had his reason. "Spoiler alert. Spider-Man dies in this one," he said as he pulled the trigger.

The .22-caliber bullet soared through the air and struck Salem right in the throat. He wasn't expecting that at all. He was thinking he was going to get shot in the leg again and was prepared for that pain. When the shot entered his neck, Salem felt his throat close as he struggled for air. He stumbled backward, holding his neck, gasping for precious oxygen, and fell over. His weight hit the decrepit tin, and he fell through, bringing half of the roof's structure crumpling on top of him.

It all happened so fast, and the bystanders stood with their mouths opened as half of the house seemed to collapse. Dust flew up and formed a cloud as wood and tin shrapnel rained down the hole that Salem's body made and buried him within the wreckage. After the noise of the demolition ceased, they realized what they had done.

Brandon took off running first, followed by Jontai, Scott, and Quinten. Dontarious stood there for a second longer, waiting for a sign of life that never came. Finally, out of panic, he took off running and joined his friends as they navigated the path back to civilization.

They never spoke a word about what happened that afternoon. They never saw Salem again, either, but since they didn't see the coverage on the news or hear reports about him missing, they figured that he was okay. They figured that he moved away out of embarrassment . . . or maybe he really was dead, and nobody gave a fuck to look for him. Either way, they never spoke of it and continued with their merry little lives.

Dontarious pushed the events to the back of his mind in a small room, locked in a safe to never be opened again. He soon forgot about his friend and nearly fourteen years went by as that day became a distant memory.

Hide-N-Seek

"Just like that, huh?" Neka asked from the far end of the couch.

Jontai stood up and grabbed his coat from the arm of the recliner. He knew the pot of shit that she was trying to stir, so he ignored her bait as he headed down the hallway. Slowly he twisted the doorknob and peeked in at his sleeping child. Not many things made Jontai smile, but seeing his son, his heir, sleeping peacefully without a worry in the world, brought a level of elation to him. He carefully closed the door and turned to head back through the living room, but Neka was standing in his path with her hands on her hips, and a bowlegged posture of sass.

"I *know* you heard me," she said as she sucked her teeth and stared a hole in his face.

Jontai brushed past her and tried to hurry to the door to avoid the imminent argument. Neka stayed breathing down his neck whenever he was about to leave the house. He thought moving out from under his mother's roof would free him, but reality brought him under the mercy of another woman: his child's mother.

Things weren't going well for Jontai. Life hadn't been easy on him, or fair, as he would sometimes put it. After high school, when the double doors opened and all of the students stepped out into the stale air of realism and responsibility, Jontai became lost in the crowd. Some kids headed for college. Some hit the job force and made a decent living while attending classes at the community college. Some climbed in the back of a Humvee and joined the armed forces. Jontai just stood there as everyone, including his friends, moved on with their life. He remained stagnant, stuck, and struck with indecisiveness and regret for all of the years that he wasted playing gangsta. Now it was his only choice.

"Let me tell you something," Neka barked as she applied a band to her ponytail and followed him to the door.

"What, Neka? Damn!" Jontai snapped as he spun and faced her.

His dreads swung from the rubber band that held them in place as he twisted his body. His voice startled her, but she was used to it. Her rage came rushing back to her vocal cords, but she tried her best to restrain herself. They were now standing inside the kitchen, and there were plenty of sharp objects for her to select from, but she just dropped her head, shook it, and chuckled a bit as she rubbed her hand across her forehead.

"You're sad, just a sad-ass nigga. You know that?" Neka asked rhetorically as she lifted her head.

Jontai turned and opened the door. It was obvious that she was looking for a fight, but he had more pertinent obligations on his mind, and arguing with Neka wasn't going to make him any money. "You come here, in my house . . ." She paused and let her words sink in as a reminder and a warning to him. "And treat it like a fucking pit stop. You just swing through when you feel like it, just to eat, wash yo' nasty ass, beg for some pussy or money, and hold your kid for like thirty minutes. Then you leave with this smug look on your face like you accomplished something. Headed back to those fucking streets, to do what? Huh? Let me know, 'cause, dammit, I'm more lost than a bitch right now." Neka waited for an answer as she cocked her head to the side.

"Neka, you know what I'm out here doing. Trying to get this money so I can take care of mines. Why you standing there acting stupid and trying to carry a nigga?"

He still held the door cracked open as a gust of the night air crept inside and cooled the sweat on his cheeks but flickered the flint of rage within Neka.

"That's just it, Jontai! I'm tired of carrying yo' bum ass!"

Her words hit hard, and the pain was evident in his eyes as he grinded his teeth. He knew that he was fucked up, but hearing it out loud, out of the mouth of someone who should've understood his situation, hurt. He felt her sharp words soar across the kitchen like rusty African spears and pierce his heart, giving him lockjaw. The truth cut deep, and the embarrassment of having your lady call you a failure as a man, lover, and father was sea salt on a marinating wound. Jontai shook his head and turned to exit the house.

"See! When shit gets real, you wanna just leave. That's your answer for—"

The sound of the screen door slamming against the frame cut her off. She pushed it open and stood on the porch barefoot as Jontai marched in shame across the yard toward his vehicle. Correction: *her* vehicle.

"You can't run away from everything, Jontai. You can't just be quiet about it, never speak on it, and just sweep it under a fucking rug thinking it will disappear."

He waved his hand over his shoulder and hopped into the Honda Accord. Her words were still floating through the air. She was still firing her tongue with bullets of truth across the yard. Lights flicked on in the neighboring houses, but they should've grown used to Jontai and Neka's reality show by then. He looked at her and turned the radio up to muffle out her words. Neka watched in anger as the car backed out of the driveway.

"One day somebody is going to lift that rug and expose the truth to you, nigga! Watch!" she shouted as she stomped her feet on the wooden surface and stormed back into the house.

Jontai parked his car alongside the curb and looked out of the window as the engine died. Under the gazebo he could see the silhouettes of a few of his workers pulling night shift. Cloverdale wasn't a cash cow by any means, and, in fact, he barely squeezed enough milk from the few local fiends to keep his team happy and somewhat loyal. He knew it wouldn't last, though. Eventually, the youngsters would wise up and move on to a different neighborhood, a more lucrative employment under the wings of a more successful dealer. Until then, he had to clock in and keep the little change flowing in his wishing well.

He stepped out of the vehicle and gave his eyes a moment to adjust to the dark environment. The lamps that were designed to illuminate the basketball court had failed to switch on that night, so the park had a gloomy vibe to it, but that was home. Since he was a junior in high school, Jontai had sat under that very gazebo and sold anything that he could market. He knew the landscape well enough to walk it blindly, and that's exactly what he did. With no hopes of a future, he lived for the present.

As he made his way to the gazebo in the center of the park, he couldn't stop the echo of Neka's words from bouncing around in his head. She always had a smart mouth and rarely bit her tongue, but there was just something about what she said that night that cut deeper than usual. He hated having his cards pulled, and she loved playing the role of a dealer—a dealer who loved calling him out on playing the role of dealer. Jontai's thoughts started to confuse him as he shook his head.

"Wuddup with it?" Jontai greeted, as he got closer to his team.

They didn't have faces. They were all hooded up, and the only light in the area was the orange pulse from the ends of their cigarettes. Jontai sat on one of the benches and looked around as he pulled a sack from his crotch.

"Ain't shit, big homie. Slow night," a voice answered. "Feel like the Dale is dying, ya feel me?"

Jontai nodded his head. It was true. The Dale was dying, and he felt like he was rotting away with it, but he was the captain of that old ship, and he planned on riding it into the waves.

"I feel ya. Y'all gon' head and bounce then. It don't seem like nobody making any noise tonight," Jontai ordered.

It was a slow night by the looks of it, but that's not why he sent them away. He really just wanted to be alone, left with his thoughts as he tried to figure out another scheme to get him to tomorrow.

"You sure you good out here dolo?" a voice asked as they all stood to their feet in sync, like a boy band.

"Yeah, I'm straight. I stay with that hammer, and you know that," Jontai said as he felt his waist, but he was lying—he had left his pistol in the car like a rookie. He watched as his troops disappeared into the shadows, and he felt his waist again, just to make sure. With everything that had happened earlier, the slick comments of a slimy grip of reality, he had caught himself slipping. He wasn't too worried at the moment. Cloverdale was his turf, and a dead zone. Nobody in their right mind would dare come at him. Not because of his false street cred, but because the entire city knew that he wasn't holding figures like that. Still, he felt uneasy being naked in the dark. He rubbed his palm over his dreads and let out a sigh. At that moment, his phone started vibrating in his pocket and made him flinch. He had to smile at his paranoia.

Jontai pulled his phone out and squinted at the bright screen. He sucked his teeth when he saw Neka's name and hit Ignore. The last thing he needed at that moment was another lecture from her. He pulled a pack of cigarettes from his other pocket and used the light from his screen to look inside. He only had three smokes left and a quarter of a blunt from earlier. As his phone started vibrating again, he reached in and lit the blunt; he would need the tranquility for the upcoming conversation.

"'Sup?" he answered as he held the smoke in his lungs.

"Somebody came by for you," Neka started out.

Jontai released the smoke as his eyes watered, and he fought back a cough. "What you mean? Who?" he asked, not sure if he heard her correctly.

Nobody ever came to her house looking for him, so the company was random and put his paranoia back on alert.

"I dunno who, nigga, but I'll tell you what I *do* know. I know you better not be having no damn fiends coming to my house no fucking more. Keep that shit out in Cloverdale with the rest of you hoodlums," Neka said with full attitude.

"Chill," Jontai said as he pulled the final hit of the blunt and flicked it across the bench.

"Chill?"

"I mean," Jontai exhaled the smoke and switched ears, "how you know it was a fiend?"

"Nigga, 'cause I know a crackhead when I see one. That I *can* spot. Wish I could detect a sorry-ass no-good nigga from the jump, but hey, we all have our flaws, right?"

"Whatever. Is that it? 'Cause I got shit to do," Jontai said as he tried to rush her off the phone. She was killing the little buzz that he did have.

"Yeah, yeah, nigga, that's it. He said that he was coming to see you. Weirdo, crackheads will do anything for that hit, I guess. Any-fucking-ways, bye, nigga!" Neka ended the call.

Jontai heard what she said when she said it, but it took a moment for it to resonate. He had no idea who could be coming to see him, and something didn't feel right. He felt his waist again and decided to head back across the park to the car to get his pistol, just in case.

As he got back to the gazebo, he felt better, safer, calmer, but his paranoid radar still flickered within the sonar of his thoughts. He looked out across the lawn and saw a figure walking toward him. Jontai stood to his feet and walked to the edge of the gazebo. He kept his hand behind his back, gripping the handle of the 9 mm he had tucked for security.

"Yo, who dat?" he asked.

His voice floated through the quiet environment, but the figure remained silent as he approached closer. He had to have heard him, and at that moment, he started feeling the hairs on the back of his neck levitate. Jontai took a step back, and finally the figure came to light.

"Mannn, nigga, don't be walking up all quiet and shit! Scared the fuck outta me!" Jontai said as he sat down on the bench and pulled his sack out. "Wuddup, Marvin?" For a second he wondered how Neka did not know who Marvin was, but he brushed the idea off.

The fiend stepped under the gazebo and pulled the white earphones out and tucked them in his ruffled collar. "You holding, Tai?"

"I got you. What you need?" Jontai said as he used the moonlight to wave his finger through his package.

"Lemme get a dub for nineteen," Marvin said as he rubbed his graying beard.

Jontai shook his head, but he made the sale. Nineteen dollars was better than what he came out there with, so he couldn't complain too much. Marvin took the rock and stuffed it in his breast pocket.

"Good looking. Y'all be easy out here," he said as he reinserted his headphones and left. Again, it took a few seconds for the words to filter through Jontai's brain.

"Y'all?" Jontai questioned as he turned around and looked under the gazebo. A figure was sitting on the far bench with a hoodie on and head low.

"Yo, who the fuck is that?" Jontai asked as he stood to his feet and reached for his pistol.

The figure remained still but finally spoke. "Is that any way to greet an old friend?"

"My nigga, you better show your face before I make it so nobody will ever recognize yo' ass!"

Jontai shouted as he raised the pistol and took aim.

"You already did that," the figure spoke calmly.

Jontai squinted his eyes, but he still couldn't get a glimpse of the person's identity. Surely one of his workers wouldn't play such a game.

"You should learn your weapons, if you're going to carry them."

"What?" Jontai asked.

Finally he was tired and a bit spooked by the riddles. He grabbed the slide of the weapon and racked it back to chamber a round, but the slide locked back, indicating that the weapon was empty. Jontai looked at it in disbelief. He knew that he had put a fresh clip in it that morning.

"That way, you'd know from the weight alone that the gun was empty," the figure said as he stood to his feet. He stepped closer as Jontai took a step back. "You and your friends tried to murder me. You left me alone to die in the woods and carried on with your merry little lives."

Jontai's mouth fell open, but he knew it couldn't be true. It couldn't be who he thought it was, not after fourteen years.

"Next time you kill somebody, make damn sure they're dead. Do you know who I am now, Jontai?"

The figure removed his hood, and Jontai's heart slid down his rib cage and dissolved in his stomach acid.

"Salem?" Jontai whispered as he took another step backward.

The person resembled the young boy that Jontai had shot in the throat that day, but it couldn't have been him. It just couldn't. Salem's dark skin and shaved head glimmered under the moonlight. He seemed as if he had barely aged, but the pain in his eyes was timeless. He stepped closer and caused Jontai to panic.

"Die for good this time, Salem, nigga!" Jontai screamed as he swung the pistol for Salem's head.

Right when he expected to feel contact, he felt something grab his arm midstrike. Salem smiled, and with a brutal yet strategic twist, he shattered the bones in Jontai's wrist, sending him kneeling to the cement floor of the gazebo as the pistol fell from his quivering grip. Jontai's scream flooded the air and instigated a smile on Salem's lips.

Jontai wasn't going down without a fight, or so he told himself. With Salem still holding his wrist, he stood to his feet and swung a wild haymaker with his left. Salem ducked it, twisted Jontai's arm behind his back, and shoved him face-first into the wood beam of the gazebo.

Jontai's nose broke on impact as blood poured out like a shattered levee. Salem pinned his face there, grabbed a fistful of Jontai's dreads, cocked his head back, and rammed it into the beam multiple times until Jontai's yelps dissolved into grunts of pure agony. The excruciating pain almost knocked him unconscious as he collapsed to the ground and rolled over on his back. The blood stopped his nose up as he gasped for air.

Salem delivered a kick into Jontai's side with his steel-toe boot, and the sound of his rib breaking echoed like a falling tree. Salem kicked him again, and again, and then stomped his chest until he felt satisfied with the misery that Jontai was experiencing. He then walked away. Jontai heard his footsteps fade and figured that it was over. He could barely move, but he swore that when he got back 100 percent he was going to finish what he should've fourteen years prior.

The sound of the footsteps returning cancelled his threat. Salem knelt beside Jontai's head, holding his pistol. He smiled and pulled a single round from his pocket and placed it in the chamber before sending the slide back forward. "You should lock your car doors, Jontai. There's some bad people in this city."

Jontai tried to sit up on his elbows, but he could only move his neck. "One thing that we have in common, my dear friend," Salem said as he grabbed Jontai's dreads and lifted his head up. He pointed the gun and pressed it against his crooked nose. ". . . is that nobody will miss either of us," Salem said with a smile.

Jontai murmured something, and Salem leaned his ear closer to listen to his prey's final plea.

"Say what?" Salem asked as he repositioned himself and leaned a knee into Jontai's broken rib.

Jontai gasped as saliva and blood leaked from the corner of his mouth. "I have a son," Jontai croaked.

Salem frowned his face up and looked around in disbelief. "Really, my nigga? You gon' pull the old, 'I have a wife and three kids' shit? You really got me fucked up if you think I care about your loved ones."

Jontai tried to squirm free, but his muscles failed him. "I'll tell you what, though. I'll spare your son. I'll wait, let him grow up until he's old enough to understand who his daddy was and what happened here tonight. And then, when he is coherent to the ways of this fucked-up world and thinks that he has life all figured out, I'll take it from him. You two can hold hands in hell."

Salem offered a sadistic grin as he jammed the pistol against Jontai's throat.

Jontai looked up. He could see Salem more clearly under the moonlight now. On Salem's neck he saw a long scar that went from ear to ear. Stitch marks surrounded it as a sign of surgery. Salem smiled when he noticed what Jontai was staring at.

"Some scars never heal," Jontai heard him say right before the flash and a serene darkness swallowed him.

Sleeping Lions

"All right, all right, all right," Grainger said as he sat on the edge of a table in the precinct break room.

His audience was a few junior officers who sat in a semicircle around him and listened googly-eyed. He wasn't used to the fame, but embraced it with opened arms as the youngsters looked up to him like he was a legendary cop of Rock City.

"So, we are on the rooftop, right? And the killer has the gun to the boy's head like this," Grainger said as he demonstrated with hand gestures. "He then points the weapon at the girl and tells her that if she doesn't kill herself, he's going to kill her brother."

"Where was your gun, Detective?" a young rookie with a close cut asked from the front row.

They all sat around like it was preschool story time; even a few old colleagues stepped in to listen to the story for the hundredth time. Grainger was once an outcast in the department and looked down on for being a fuckup. For once, he was getting the respect and admiration that he rightfully deserved, and he was soaking up the shine like sunrays on pale skin.

"The killer had my gun. I had to hand it over when I showed up at the scene." At first, reciting the story was difficult for Grainger, but as the months went by, he slowly adjusted to the expectations and became more comfortable. What was once a life-threatening event had transformed into a motivational speech.

"Man! Were you scared? You had a vest on, right, Detective?" a blue-eyed female with short dark hair asked from the middle of the crowd.

"Nope. You have to remember, I wasn't on duty. I wasn't even supposed to be there."

Ohs and *ahs* circulated around the room for the rebel cop-turned-rock star. His story of redemption inspired a lot of knucklehead badges to turn their careers around.

"Damn, you're a brave one," somebody commented.

Grainger was feeling himself then. He stood up from the edge of the desk and really started getting into his story.

"So we are up there for a while. Arguing back and forth like a married couple, ya know? And finally the young girl says 'fuck it.' She picks the gun up and puts it to her head." He pointed his finger to his temple and surveyed the suspense of his listeners. "Then she pulls the tri—"

"Grainger!" a voice shouted from across the room.

Grainger looked up and saw Detective Miller standing in the doorway with a half-eaten apple in his hand. He took a bite out of it and nodded toward the exit. "Let's go . . . Bring ya' ass."

"A'ight, let me finish this up," Grainger said as he waved Miller off. "So she's holding the revolver to her head and—"

"Grainger! Stop telling your fucking war stories and let's go. We have a call," Miller said sharply as he tossed the apple into a trash can.

He still didn't care too much for his young trigger-happy partner and did a poor job of suppressing it. Grainger shook his head and stepped away from the table. He looked at the crowd and adjusted his maroon tie over his plain white shirt.

"Sorry, class. We'll continue this at another time. Somebody pissed in Poppa Bear's porridge." Sighs of disappointment filled the room as Grainger walked toward the door. "Don't worry; it's in my files. Go read it," he said to the crowd as he walked past Miller.

As he was walking through the department, a rookie cop named Timothy Cherry dashed in front of him, stalling his stride. "Detective," he started with a smile and rubbed his hand over his high-top fade. "Aye, I don't wanna seem like I'm dick-riding, you feel where I'm coming from, but—" he cut himself off and chuckled. The black male with a baby face and thick lips adjusted his uniform. He wasn't young and was actually around Grainger's age, but new to the force after a late rocky start. "I was wondering if we can get together later. Ya know, maybe I can pick your brain a little, and you can give me a few pointers. See, I'm just like you," Officer Cherry leaned closer. "I'm a fucked-up black cop who is looking for a new light. You're like an idol to the rest of us here. You," he poked Grainger in the chest and smiled, but quickly returned his face to a serious posture, "you proved that the past doesn't matter, and no grave is too deep to bounce out of, ya know. Whenever you're ready . . ." Grainger was flattered and placed a hand on the officer's shoulder.

"I got you, Cherry. Let me go handle this right quick and we'll sit down. I feel your pain. I've been there, brother." Officer Cherry smiled and walked away.

Grainger could get used to the glamour and the newfound leadership. A number of cops had been approaching him, and at first, it felt weird, but now, thanks to his dark shades of confidence, the limelight wasn't that bad.

Lately, Grainger had been feeling like Mike Lowrey from *Bad Boys*. He closed a crucial case, received many accolades from the department, and now his once-shaky career was on a solid foundation.

He stopped at a young officer's desk, a brown-skinned female with hazel contacts and jet-black hair named Shona. She looked up and batted her long eyelashes at him as he sat at the edge of her desk.

"Hey, gorgeous," he flirted innocently. Before she could respond, Miller walked by and snatched Grainger up by his tie.

"Stop fucking around and let's go!" Miller barked as he seemed to drag him through the office and out the front door.

"Damn, what's your problem?" Grainger said once they were outside. He turned around to adjust his tie and look at his reflection in the mirror-tinted door. He saw Miller's reflection mystically appear over his shoulder.

"*You're* my fucking problem. You're going around here parading like you are big shit!"

Miller said as he walked toward their unmarked car and climbed in. Grainger hopped in the passenger seat and grabbed his Monster from the cup holder. He cracked it open and turned the can up to his lips.

"You need to relax, Miller. I'm just enjoying myself. I'm in a good space right now," Grainger said as he placed the energy drink down. It was warm, but it hit the spot. He consumed so many of them that he rarely noticed the spike of energy that the label promised.

"Relax? Let me tell you something."

Grainger rolled his eyes. He knew he was in for another lecture from his seasoned partner.

Miller scratched the side of his graying head and navigated the vehicle out of the parking lot. "You have a lot to learn, Dontarious. You think that closing one case is something to be proud of? You *really* think that? Negro, please! That ain't shit. It doesn't make you a fucking hero, and it damn sure don't make you a legend. You keep letting those pats on the back push you forward, and you're going trip over your own shoes."

Miller accelerated wildly and weaved in and out of traffic. He flashed his sirens at red lights and sped right through.

"If I didn't know any better, I'd swear you were becoming a hater," Grainger joked as he took another sip.

"A *hater*? Of what? Boy, you must really have lost your damn mind!"

"I'm just joking," Grainger started as he waved his hand to dismiss the conversation from escalading. He always seemed to forget that Miller wasn't issued a sense of humor from the department.

"I was putting murders away when your little ass was still playing Hide-N-Seek. You better get your facts straight, youngin'. Ask these damn streets about Miller. I've given out more passes than you have arrests . . . In fact, you don't even have any arrests! Every assailant you go up against ends up dead! And you got the scrotum to call yourself a legendary cop?"

Grainger was quiet for a few awkward minutes as the facts sank into his skull. "That's cold, partner."

"Nah, that's *real*. This city is cold. Listen, the murders don't stop just 'cause you close a case, remember that. Every morning, it's a new case. You better humble yourself, or these streets will do it for you," Miller said as he pointed his finger at Grainger.

"Anyway," Grainger said as he looked out the window, "what's the call about?"

"Like any other," Miller's voice was calm now. "It rained last night, so new bodies are sprouting up."

Grainger was shocked when they pulled into Cloverdale and stopped near the crime scene that used to be a park. He grew up in that neighborhood. He hung out under that very gazebo, scraped his knee on that very court, smoked his first cigarette behind the bushes, and kissed his first lips under the slide. Cloverdale was home, and the fact that a body had appeared that close to the steps of his childhood messed with him a little.

They exited the car and made their way up to the gazebo. Cops were everywhere, looking for clues, or at least acting like they were. Sergeant Rollins, Grainger's sworn enemy on the force, was in charge of the scene. He looked over his shoulder and met them at the edge of the gazebo. A body was lying in the grass with a black tarp covering it. Grainger looked around and tried to fight off the emotions of seeing blood on his home turf. All he could think about was the route that he had taken to avoid dying in that park; now he was responding to clean up a scene of a fellow native.

"Dontarious!" Rollins greeted with artificial excitement.

He hated Grainger but loved getting under his skin, and lately, with Grainger's new fame, Rollins wanted nothing more than to become a cancerous parasite. He was a muscular figure with blond, spikey hair that didn't match his age, and a douche bag tan that could only honor the cast of *Jersey Shore*. He was holding on to his high school dreams, looks, and bullylike demeanor.

"Welcome home! As you can see, we threw you a little party, you hero," Rollins said as he nudged Grainger.

Miller squatted by the body and pulled the tarp back. Grainger nearly pulled a leapfrog maneuver as he rushed over to see if his eyes were playing tricks on him. Rollins saw the look on his distraught face and saw a lane to fuck with him on a personal level. He walked over with a bop as he chuckled and snapped his fingers. "Let me guess . . . One of your old homies?" Rollins said as he winked his fingers.

Grainger couldn't believe he was looking at Jontai's corpse with a hole in his neck and burgundy-stained grass beneath him like cheap shag carpet from the '70s. It took him a minute to get his thoughts together. Everyone knew that Jontai was a piece of shit, and he'd never amount to anything more than that with his chosen lifestyle, but Grainger never wanted to see him dead. They hadn't spoken in years, mainly because a fence of justice separated their lifestyles. With that aside, Grainger sorrowed for the loss of an old friend.

"As a matter of fact, he is," Grainger said as he turned away and looked across the park. The entire block seemed to be outside staring at the scene—mainly just nosy people trying to catch a peek of who had met his demise.

"Any witnesses?" Grainger asked as he rubbed his hand over his low cut.

He knew the answer to that question already, but asked it anyway out of formality. Nobody spoke to the cops in Cloverdale, not willingly, at least. And with all the heat that police officers were catching worldwide, no civilians were looking to make their jobs any easier.

Rollins chuckled. "What do you think? We did find dope on him, of course. So you know what that means, right?" Rollins stepped closer with a grin on his pink lips. "Drug related. So your little homie back there is going to get swept under a rug."

Grainger looked at him and wanted to break his nose. He had to tell himself that it wasn't worth it. His career was finally out of the hole, and he'd be damned if he let Rollins bring him back down with words. His fist automatically tightened up, but he restrained himself and tucked his hands in the pockets of his slacks.

Grainger followed Miller back to the squad car. Standing on the curb near their vehicle, he saw a familiar face that locked eyes with him and dropped his head. It struck Grainger as odd so he approached him.

"Marvin? What's up? You got this look on your face like you know something about what happened here," he said as he stood in front of him. Marvin looked around and stepped off the curb.

"I'm a fiend, but I'm not a snitch," he said, making sure everyone around him could hear it.

The last thing Marvin needed was a killer after him for running his mouth, or the next dealer to banish him getting his next hit—but Marvin couldn't help but feel bad for Jontai. He had just seen him a few hours ago; that fact alone fucked with him.

"Snitches are people who give up information to save their own ass. You're not in trouble, so giving me a lead in this case would only be considered doing the right thing for the safety of your community." Grainger politicked.

An older lady with a crooked wig and pink house slippers stood behind Marvin. She leaned forward and whispered something to him and pushed him forward. He was hesitant as he looked around and lowered his voice. "Look, Jontai was a good dude, and I think it's real fucked-up what happened here. All I know is that I saw him last night, and he was sitting right there under that thingamajig with some strange-acting dude in a hoodie. I swear that's all I saw," Marvin said as he walked back and stood on the curb. Grainger nodded his appreciation and hopped in the passenger seat.

"Whelp, that's that," Miller said as he pulled off.

Grainger snapped his head toward him as they made a careful three-point turn. "What do you mean? Oh, so when it's black-on-black or some shit go down in a black neighborhood, it's no longer a case, huh? Just mark it off as drug related? You're no better than that fucking Rollins."

Grainger's attitude stemmed deeper than Rollins's comments and sowed around wild thoughts in his head like roots. He couldn't help but feel guilty for not at least trying to steer Jontai away from that lifestyle. Even as adults, they were apples and oranges, and it had been that way since they were teens . . . plums and tangerines.

"Listen, it ain't about black-on-black, or white, or brown, or even fucking purple. When bacteria kills off bacteria, we consider that a cure."

Grainger couldn't believe what he was hearing. He had to stare at his partner for a second and let the comment register. Miller's old ass, of all people, should be ashamed of saying such a thing. Grainger had to give him the elevator look, just to ensure that Rollins wasn't the one talking to him—it sounded like a racist remark that he would proudly say.

"You sound retarded! Murder is still murder, or have you forgotten? A witness back there said that he saw our victim sitting with a man in a hoody. I'm willing to bet my bottom dollar that's our suspect. That's who we need to be looking for."

Miller slowed the car down and looked at Grainger as if he'd lost his mind. "No, *that* sounds retarded! Look!" He pointed out the window toward the crowd lined up on the curb and lawns. "Look right there. That little boy has on a hoodie. Want to arrest him? What about that lady in the pink one? Want to bring her in for questioning? Look at that big, tall, black muthafucka in the middle there with a hoodie.

Is *he* our guy?" Miller asked as he paused so
his point could get across, and then stomped
the gas. "Your bottom dollar ain't worth shit
in this city. If a working-class man was in that
park dead, I might be obliged to feel something
for the case. But a drug dealer? I'd say Karma
solved the case for us."

Grainger felt where he was coming from and
realized that he didn't have a solid lead, but he
wasn't ready to give up on his friend's killer. He
turned in his seat and looked back at the last guy
that Miller pointed out, but he had faded into
the crowd. There was something about him . . .

Salem vanished into the crowd and watched
as his work brought havoc to the neighborhood. He had his hoodie pulled tightly and
walked with his head low to avoid detection.
He really didn't have to, because everyone was
too busy being nosy to notice him lurking in
his sheep's clothing. He found a good spot in
the shadows and waited. He looked around
at the familiar faces and despised them. They
seemed mighty interested in the death of a
drug dealer, but nobody gave a fuck when he
went missing as a teen. Nobody! Not even his
best friend. Nobody gave a fuck when he had

to go live with his grandmother, in some sort of fucked-up parody of *The Fresh Prince of Bel-Air*. Nobody gave a fuck when he turned up missing in Afghanistan. Nobody gave a fuck, and now he was back in the city to take it.

His heartbeat increased when he saw the cop car pull up and a familiar face hop out of the passenger seat. Salem watched and tried his best to fight off his laughter as Dontarious walked around dumbfounded to his fate. Seeing his face turn to stone when he was shown Jontai's body almost made Salem burst into tears of joy. After Dontarious climbed back into the car and pulled off, Salem made sure to make his way to curb as close as he could. He wanted him to see him. He wanted to see Dontarious up close and connect eyes like destined soul mates of death. Their eyes did lock, but Grainger seemed spaced out. Salem smiled and floated back into the crowd in case the risky move had blown his cover.

"See you soon, old friend. The lion has awakened."

Double Dutch

Neka sat in her living room with the TV on mute and her thoughts on blast. Sandalwood incense burned slowly in the far corner on a small oak table, but her spirit was cold and long depleted of a spark. The smoke detector in the hallway beeped every three minutes as a warning of a low battery, but her brain cells were fully charged and alert to her recent pain which was ablaze. She never truly admitted her appreciation for Jontai to his face, or even in her head, but in his wake, she regretted every second that she slept on their potential dreams of happiness.

She tucked her feet beneath her and pulled a few strands of her medium-length hair; then she bit down on her full lips and frowned at how dry they were. She wiped her face directly under her eye sockets and frowned at how damp it was. She held her chest, and beneath her breast she could feel a rapid heartbeat in the quiet room, causing her to frown at her level of anxiety. She was lost.

Ever since she received the news of his murder, she couldn't help but think of her last words to him. She frowned at how harsh they were.

For days she sat in a funk . . . regret's fragrance of a broken heart. She even had to send her child to her mother, because her current state as a weak, disheartened street widow made her unfit for the athletic responsibilities of raising a child. *This is temporary. This too shall pass. That nigga deserved what he got,* she told herself. "Damn, I miss him so much," she admitted in a faint voice as she stood and stretched her legs.

She hadn't left the house all day, but she was dressed like she had plans. Her cell phone stayed vibrating until it eventually died. She wasn't in the mood to speak to anyone, or see anyone, and seemed as if everyone and their momma, including her momma's momma, was calling to check up on her. It wasn't that serious, she lied to herself—just another trifling-ass nigga that was caught slipping in Karma's trust fall.

A knock at her door startled her from her thoughts. She turned her head toward it, but her body remained still. She waited to see if the knock would come again. A part of her was hoping that her ears were just playing tricks on her and no one was there. Another part of her hoped that someone was there, someone comforting, that she could run to and bury her face into a caring chest and drain her septic eyes of the bullshit. Another part of her was hoping that it was him. That part of her was crazy, but the thought was entertaining at least, as her misery was beginning to tear her apart.

The knock returned. Paranoia swept across her mind and stopped just long enough to drop off a terrorizing thought. *What if the killer is looking for me now?* She shook her head and walked toward the door. As she passed the kitchen counter, she grabbed her pocketknife . . . just in case.

She glanced through the peephole and saw the familiar face of an old friend. She was glad to see her but didn't know if she really wanted to deal with her that night. Neka paused as she grabbed the doorknob to unlock it. She considered sneaking away on her tiptoes and faking sleep, but the lonely part of her took control of her hand and opened the door.

"This bitch here," Toni said as she welcomed herself inside.

She stood at five foot eight, had mocha skin with slanted eyes that she kept outlined in bright eye shadow for emphasis, and she stayed decked out in an exotic weave that never stopped anywhere less than the small of her back. Her apparel alone spoke volumes of her persona. She was about money and chased the currents of the financial river to whatever banks it led.

She and Neka had history in college and remained close a short time afterward. It wasn't until Neka gave birth to her son that their relationship started to fade. Toni was still big on the club scenes, barhopping, man thirsty, and chasing cheap thrills in expensive shoes. Neka was forced to calm down and be a mother. She didn't regret her sudden birth of maturity, but sometimes she did miss the life that Toni mastered.

"So we don't answer phones now? We just sit up in the dark with candles burning and ignore our day-one bitches?" Toni asked with attitude as she surveyed the living room and turned to Neka.

"Yes, you may enter," Neka said as she still held the door open and pretended to be shocked at Toni's forwardness.

"Please," Toni said as she sucked her teeth.

She flicked on a light switch in the kitchen, forcing Neka to cover her eyes for a second as they adjusted. "I know one thing . . . You better get out of your feelings and move on with your life," Toni said as she navigated to the living room and flopped on the couch. "Life is too short to be stressing over some nigga. Believe me, I know."

Neka looked at her and shook her head as she entered the living room and sat across from her in the recliner. "You talking like I just got dumped. My dude was murdered. I dunno if you got the memo or did the street rumors twist the story up?"

"I know that, but what now?" Toni asked as she spread her arms in her sleeveless top. "What are you going do? Mope around this bitch until God sends you another man? Or are you gon' put your big-bitch panties on and handle your business for your seed?"

"I'm handling mines, Toni. Don't get it fucked up," Neka said as she grabbed the remote and unmuted the TV. She flipped through the channels as if she was actually interested in finding something. In actuality, the topic of the conversation was making her uncomfortable. Toni had a way of downplaying serious situations, and had been that way since college; it was nothing short of a miracle that she made it out.

"Where is the little man at anyway? Asleep?" Toni asked as she pulled her phone from her purse.

"With my mom," Neka responded.

Her mind drifted away as she wondered what her little munchkin was up to. She called to speak to him earlier, as if he could really talk, but his grunts and giggles confirmed that he was still alive and doing okay. He was still smiling like sunrays piercing the dark cloud that hovered over her life. In time, the misery would pass, but until then, Neka remained still, gripping an emotional umbrella, waiting to be struck by a bolt of reality.

"Well, shit, let's get it then!" Toni shouted excitedly. Nothing would've pleased her more than hitting the town with her girl like old times.

"What you mean?" Neka looked over and saw the anticipation on Toni's face. She knew what she was getting at, but she played dumb to buy her time to format an excuse.

"For old time's sake, let me take you out, get a drink, and catch up with each other. Shit, you already dressed. It seems like destiny to me," Toni said and signed it with a smile.

"Or fate," Neka said as she rolled her eyes.

"What else are you gonna do? Sit up in this bitch? Adopt a few dozen cats? Start knitting? Work on that next American novel? Bitch, please. Let's enjoy these moments. If we are going to take anything from this situation, it should be that life is short."

Neka had to admit Toni had a point. She was already dressed. She could go for a strong drink and fresh air. Life *is* short, and she needed to stand tall against the medium of tribulation. "Okay. Fuck it. Okay, I'm with it," Neka said reluctantly.

"Good, let's get to it," Toni said as she stood to her feet and clinched her purse. Neka grabbed her purse as well and tossed her pocketknife inside, just in case.

"I have one stop to make first, if that's okay," Toni announced as she adjusted her hair in a small mirror.

"Oh Gawd, some nigga, huh?" Neka knew her too well. "Don't you still date some little square-ass nigga that lives in the city with yo' digging ass?"

"Of course. I love my boo Q. But tonight, I'm going to check out this other nigga I met last week."

Neka shook her head. Toni still had dollar bills on her mind and hadn't changed a bit. She coined lust over wishing wells and fairy tales of finding that hood quarterback and not some lame benchwarmer that was still nickel-and-diming.

"He might got some friends. Want me to ask? I mean, if you with it?" Toni said as they made their way across the yard and got into her Tahoe.

"Bitch, fuck no. I can almost guarantee if a nigga fuck with yo' trifling ass, I wouldn't want anything to do with one of his fucked-up-ass friends."

The two women exited the elevator and walked in silence down the dimly lit hallway. Neka trailed Toni while her thoughts of regret weighed in on her shoulders. She was tired and didn't really notice until she started moving around. Now she was on another "Toni Adventure." Her spirit and joints weren't as young and enthused as they once were in her college days. Instead of being excited about hitting the town, Neka was busy thinking about being home on her couch, inside the peaceful confines of her living room—surrounded by dead thoughts. Now she was following Toni to meet one of her fuck buddies; Neka really didn't have the vigor for the upcoming scene.

Scott heard a knock at the door and jogged down the hallway of his apartment in his basketball shorts and tight tank top. His muscular arms were exposed, but his light skin was buried under the sleeves of ink that he had collected over the years.

Scott had done well for himself after high school and moved on like the rest of the old crew.

He attended Winston Salem State, made new friends, broke new hearts of young women, and eventually graduated with a major in business and a minor in deceit. He took his education and combined it with his lust for women, and opened a clothing store that catered to the latest female trends.

His business was doing okay, about as good as any small establishment in a small town could do in its first few years, and he was happy. He had access to his first love besides money: pussy. And it seemed to just walk through the doors and throw itself on the counter. Next, he wanted to open a salon, but Rock City wasn't big enough for him; Scott had dreams of taking over Raleigh or Greensboro, but those dreams were pushed left until he got his money right.

He opened the door and saw Toni standing in a black sleeveless top and tight jeans that bear-hugged her thick thighs. He looked her up and down as he bit down on his pink lip and rubbed his hand over his curly 'fro. He was staring at her so hard that he didn't notice Neka standing behind her until Toni stepped past him. He gave Neka a nod and returned his eyes back to Toni's ass as she walked across the living room.

Neka entered and closed the door behind her. It didn't shut all of the way and seemed to be wedged. "Oh, you gotta slam that, ma. It's a little ghetto," Scott said over his shoulder as he stalked toward Toni. He grabbed her by the waist and pulled her close as their lips locked. Neka tried to shut the door, but it proved difficult. Eventually, she sighed and leaned her shoulder into it like a football drill. When it was finally closed, she hit the lock and turned to see Toni and Scott grinding each other near the kitchen wall.

Toni opened her eyes while Scott sucked on her bottom lip and looked over his shoulder at Neka. She saw the discomfort in her face, so she pushed Scott away. "Aye, this is my girl, Neka. Neka, this is Scott." Toni introduced as she adjusted her top.

"'Sup with ya?" Scott asked as he walked over and moved a few magazines and his laptop from the couch. "Have a seat, make yourself at home. I mean . . ." He rubbed the side of his head and looked at Neka as she stood with her arms folded, which pushed her lavish breasts up higher.

He couldn't help but stare for a second. The arrogant part of his brain kicked in. He had a vulgar thought that maybe Toni had brought her girl over for a threesome.

"If you want, I can call one of my mans over to keep you company, or you good?" Scott asked as he tested the waters.

Neka sat down in the spot that he cleared on the leather couch and decided not to respond to his inquiry.

"She good, Scott. Chill," Toni said. He turned to her and looked for a hint on her face. "She lost her baby daddy the other day, so I'm taking her out tonight to cheer my bitch up. We just stopped by here so I can get what you owe me," Toni said as she licked her lips seductively.

"I'm sorry to hear that," Scott said as he smiled. "These streets are getting crazy. I was watching the news earlier and saw that one of the niggas I used to go to school with got dropped in Cloverdale. Somebody blew the Adam's apple outta his neck," Scott said as he reached for Toni's waist.

Suddenly her face changed, and she blocked his hands. He looked up at her puzzled. Neka raised her head and looked over at him to see if she heard him correctly. She could tell by the look on Toni's face that her ears were precise.

"You knew Jontai?" Neka said in an almost whisper.

Scott turned to her and tried to gauge what was going on. They were looking at him as if he had told a family secret in public.

"Yeah. That was my dude back in the day. I haven't spoke to the nigga in ages. I kinda regret that now, but . . ." Scott lowered his head when his slow mind finally caught on.

"Don't we all," Neka responded and turned her head toward the TV.

"My bad, ma. I didn't—you know, I didn't mean to." Toni grabbed his hand and pulled him closer to her.

"It's cool. Aye, you mind if I turn your TV on?" Neka asked as she grabbed the remote. She just wanted to change the subject.

She came out to escape the mourning of her child's father and ended up running into one of his old friends. The night was already getting crazy.

Toni pulled Scott down the hallway, but he looked back at Neka. He wanted to say something to her. He wanted to apologize more and offer his condolences wholeheartedly, but Toni's soft hands reaching down his shorts triggered another feeling that presided over sympathy.

She pulled him into the room and shut the door behind him as she pinned him against it. The room was dark except the rays of light that poured in from a large window next to the bed. Her soft lips connected with his as her tongue explored his mouth. As a sign of her passion, she bit down on his lip before attacking his neck in ginger kisses. She left a saliva trail to his collarbone and slid her hands up his tank top. Scott's dick bulged against the threads of his shorts, and Toni took notice as she pushed herself against it and grabbed his shaft.

She made it obvious that she came over with one thing on her mind as she dropped to her knees and yanked his shorts down. His dick stood straight out like a weed in a rock bed, but she didn't hesitate to make half of the thick muscle disappear into her hungry jaws. She lubed it up with her spit as her mouth started to water, influenced by his groans. She went deeper, until his entire dick was in her mouth and jammed into her throat. She held that position as the sensation tortured Scott. He slid over and tried to grip the dresser, but Toni went even deeper and pulled an experienced porn star move by extending her tongue and licking his balls.

As she backed off his dick slowly, a strand of saliva trailed from her lips to the head of his dick. Like rewinding a scene, she sucked the spittle back up and started bobbing on his dick mercilessly. Scott folded his hands over his head like a boss as she went to work, employed in the task of a toe-curling blowjob.

Just when he thought she was laying off, she clocked his dick back in her throat and went overtime. Her nipples got a raise from his wails of feedback. He promoted a job well done as he grabbed the back of her head and trained her to his desired speed. Right when he felt the tingling sensation in his body and he was ready to fire, she pulled back and stood to her feet. He opened his eyes for the first time in minutes and saw her drop her jeans to her ankles, and then lean over the bed. She stretched out and started jiggling her ass as a Christmas bonus.

Scott kicked his shorts from out under him and walked over to where she was lying on her stomach. He stroked his dick a few times and pulled a condom off of his nightstand. He stared at her as she continued to wobble her cheeks like chocolate waves in an ebony sea. Scott slid the condom on and got into position behind her to set sail. He rubbed the tip of his dick against moist lips of her pussy and her clit.

"Stop playing with it and take this shit!" Toni said aggressively. Scott eased inside of her slowly like he was walking the plank and immediately felt her clench her warms walls around his hard wood.

She purred as he went deeper and stroked her in a circular motion, searching for her spot. He sped up as the clapping sound of their thighs connecting echoed throughout the room. Knowing how she liked it, Scott smacked her ass, but it wasn't enough for her.

"Harder," she mumbled between moans. Scott smacked her other cheek. "Harder!" she screamed.

He cocked his hand back and delivered a thunderous smack like he was playing his last domino. Then he reached forward and grabbed her arms and held them behind her back by her wrists.

"Is *this* what you came for?" he grunted as he continued pounding.

Sweat dripped from his curly hair and spilled down his chest. Toni didn't hear a word that he uttered. A potent orgasm was charging up in her soul, and a power surge temporarily disabled her senses.

"*Huh?*" Scott demanded.

He pulled out and flipped her over to her back. As he entered her again, he grabbed her neck and began thrusting as her juices lubricated his wrath. She reached up and grabbed his hands and squeezed them tighter around her neck. Scott knew she was into some freaky shit, but never guessed that she liked to be choked.

Taking the hint, he began choking her, and stroking her, and digging deeper into her pussy as she lifted her legs into the air with her mouth wide open reaching for oxygen.

Luckily, Scott finally came and filled the tip of the condom with hot sperm. He collapsed on top of her and let go of her neck. She gasped as air rushed into her lungs and water leaked from her sockets. Scott looked up at her as her body started to shake. For a second, it scared him that he may have taken it too far and forced a seizure out of her crazy ass, so he stood up and watched her body shiver violently, like she was experiencing an exorcism.

Toni reached down and started fingering herself and rapidly played her clit like a guitar string. It was her solo, and she blacked out as she tuned her orgasm and twisted her body wildly across the mattress. This turned Scott back on. He snatched the condom off without even thinking and grabbed her waist, pulling her off the bed. She was still playing with herself, with her head rocked back.

He pushed her hand out the way, but she moved it back and continued fingering herself into another orgasm. Scott pushed her across the room and bent her over the dresser, knocking its contents onto the floor. He spread her legs and entered her like a madman. Her pussy was so wet that he could barely feel her walls, but the warmth of her canal around his bare skin was to die for.

Her moans turned to screams as he pumped in and out of her, with his balls clapping against her clit. He reached up and grabbed the back of her neck, just how she liked it. He fucked her like he hated her—just how she liked it. He sped up when he felt his nut raising to the tip of his dick and carelessly exploded all inside of her—just how she liked it.

When it was over and both of their senses returned, he eased out of her as their juices leaked down the inside of her legs. Scott sat on the edge of the bed and caught his breath. The room was getting hot, so he opened the window—oblivious of whether someone could see his naked body from the fourth floor.

Toni swiped her sweat-laced hair from her face and sat beside him on the bed as she began getting dressed. "Damn, you worse than a nigga. You just gon' smash and dash?" Scott asked as he leaned back onto the mattress. He really didn't care if she left and actually preferred it.

"Chill. You got smoke?" Toni asked. After a session like that, a blunt was the cherry on her banana split.

"Nah, but I'll buy if you go get it," he proposed.

He wasn't much of a weed smoker, but he could use another high for the night, or else he'd end up calling another girl over in a few hours. By the time Toni got back with the bud, he'd be ready to fuck again, so it was a win-win to him.

"Bet," Toni replied as she stood up and adjusted her hair in the dark room.

Scott reached in the nightstand for some cash and paused when he saw his condoms. Reality rushed back to his pores with shame beaded into sweat as he realized that he went raw on her and ejaculated inside of her. He handed her the money and leaned back on the bed as he stared at the ceiling, deep in thought.

Toni exited the room with a smile on her face; the same smile a lioness makes when it corners a victim and sees the look of despair on its face. When she entered the living room she looked over and saw Neka on the couch, passed out with her head cocked to the side. "Neka," Toni said lowly. "Neka!" she spoke a little louder. "Poor girl is exhausted."

Toni shook her head and figured she'd leave her there to sleep until she got back; then she would take her home and reschedule their night. The weed man stayed just up the street anyway. Neka's body jerked as she readjusted her head to the other side and started snoring tenderly.

Toni smirked and opened the door quietly. She grinned at her friend as she closed the door behind her gently.

Neka hadn't slept well in days, and it finally caught up to her as she sat on the couch and tried to stifle out Toni's screams with the TV. She drifted away as her eyelids lowered and her exhaustion, as well as her thoughts, took over her body. She kept replaying the same scene in her head.

She saw Jontai as he waved his hand over his shoulder and hopped into the Honda Accord. She listened as her words floated through the air. She saw herself standing on the porch as she fired her tongue with bullets of truth across the yard. She looked around and saw the lights flicker on in the neighboring houses. She watched in empathy as the car backed out of the driveway.

"One day somebody is going to lift that rug and expose the truth to you, nigga! Watch!" she heard herself shout as she stomped her bare foot on the wooden surface and stormed back into the house. Just as she blinked, Jontai appeared in her face, dressed in all-white, with his dreads lying neatly over his shoulders, and worry instilled in his eyes. He looked at her and asked a question that struck her as weird.

"Remember me?"

Neka opened her eyes, and it took a second for her to realize that she was just dreaming. Slowly, she recognized her surroundings. She turned her head left and saw Scott's door, only it wasn't closed all the way. It was jammed on the frame, as it was when she initially tried to gently close it. She looked to her right and nearly jumped out of her skin. A figure dressed in all-black was sitting next to her. She immediately recognized him as the guy that asked about Jontai on the night of his death. He offered her a callous grin as he sat with his hands in the pockets of his jacket.

"Remember me?"

Right when Neka opened her mouth to scream, he lunged forward and covered her mouth with a damp rag. The vapors of the chloroform seeped into her body and everything immediately faded.

Scott lay on his back with his arms crossed behind his head as he stared in shame at the ceiling. He couldn't believe that he was reckless enough to go raw on Toni and not even pull out. He figured that he would have to do some slick talking to her during the next few days and convince her to take the morning-after pill, or worse. He sucked his teeth when he replayed the scene in his head. His frown turned into a smile when he recollected how good the pussy was, though. He still planned on slaying her again, if it was the last thing he did.

"Aye, do you remember that time . . ." Scott heard a voice ask as the door barged open and the lights flicked on. He rubbed his eyes and looked up at the six-foot-five male as he stood in the doorway. His face slowly formed into recognition. He was older, he was bigger, but he was Salem.

"What? I have something on my face?" Salem asked as he touched his cheek. "What about my neck?" he tilted his head back and exposed the thick scar.

Scott shuffled out of the bed and stood to his feet. He was only wearing his shorts and held his fists to his side in rage. "Salem, what the fuck are you doing in my crib?" he asked as he breathed heavily.

His heart's RPMs were maxing out as he felt the rage shift gears into survival mode. He hadn't seen Salem since the day they left him in the woods, and honestly thought he'd never have to see him again. There could only be one reason that he showed up after that long . . . and it damn sure wasn't a social visit. Scott's eyes expanded when he thought about Jontai.

"Look at you. Done got some muscles and shit. Thinking you all strong now!" Salem said as he pointed at Scott's bare chest in a proud smile.

"You're about to find out just how strong I am, my nigga." Scott threatened as he scanned the room for an object that he could use as a weapon.

"Well, let's not waste time with the small talk then," Salem said as he took off his jacket and let it drop to the floor. He held his hands out in front of him and rotated his shoulders in the tight fabric of the desert-tan Under Armour shirt. "And for the record, I was never your nigga."

Scott rushed forward and swung at Salem's head. Salem ducked and delivered a punch to his gut that sent him immediately to his knees, wheezing for air. Salem walked to the other side of the room and looked out of the window calmly. "That's always been your problem, Scott. You focused your entire life on chasing pussy. You worked out and got in shape to impress women. You rented this nice apartment, with this lovely view, to impress women and both of them will be your downfall."

Scott stood to his feet and grabbed a lamp from the dresser. He snatched the cord from the wall and swung it at Salem's back, but he missed as the porcelain shattered against the window-pane. Salem elbowed him in the chest, almost as if he was careful to not damage Scott's face. Scott stumbled back, but Salem lunged forward and kicked him in the same spot with his combat boot. Scott fell over a desk as it tumbled on top of him to the floor. He hurriedly pushed it off of him and tried to stand, but he felt a sharp pain in his stomach.

Salem leaned closer and shoved the blade deeper into Scott's flesh as blood poured out and leaked down his torso. Scott screamed, but Salem kept pushing the blade farther in, and then snatched it out before he tossed the knife across the floor. He then wiped the blood from his leather gloves across Scott's chest. Scott lay there as his warm blood covered his body and pooled beneath his back. He stared at the ceiling again in regret.

Salem pulled a bundle of 550 cord from his cargo pocket and tied one end to the bed-post. Then he carefully tied a noose on the opposite end. He stood up and walked over to Scott and smiled at him as he leaned over and dragged him near the window. Scott tried to speak, but his mouth filled with blood.

"Listen, my nigga," Salem said as he lifted Scott to his nimble feet and held him in front of the open window.

He grabbed the rope and tightened it around Scott's neck. Scott stood there as he felt the life creeping from his body, basically paralyzed in sorrow's Karma. Salem gave the rope a final tug as Scott felt his airway close.

"Let's see who is Spider-Man now." Salem said as he shoved Scott's body out of the window and walked toward the door.

The rope tightened, and the bed was yanked from its position and slid toward the window with a loud snap. Scott's body hung there, his eyes still open, staring into the sky as blood leaked from his toes and dripped onto the parked cars beneath him. Slowly, his corpse swayed in the wind like the dial on a grandfather's clock. Scott's time had finally come to an end.

Marco Polo

"Edgecombe County 911, what's your emergency?"

"Hello, is this the police?"

"Yes sir. How can I be of assistance?"

"Aye, check it out, right. I'm over here in Tiffany Square Apartments, and it's like a body hanging from one of the damn windows."

"Sir, did you say a body?"

"Yeah, just hanging there. I think that nig . . . I'm sorry, I think that man is dead."

"Okay, can you tell which apartment the individual is hanging from?"

"Nah, but he up there, and he not moving. I'm 100 that he is dead as shit, feel me?"

"Okay, I'm sending responders to the scene. What's your name?"

"My name? Oh, my name is Marco, and pretty much, my job is done here. Your turn."

***

Grainger hated late-night calls. He preferred early mornings when the sun is out and the scene is less gloomy. He had his energy drink within his grip as he stepped under the crime tape and made his way to where he saw Miller standing next to two uniformed cops. They were staring up at the side of the building, and as Grainger looked up, a chill of déjà vu pulsed through his spine. He stopped beside Miller and tried to focus on the swaying body while his heart stood still.

"About time you showed up. Let's go in," Miller said as he smacked Grainger in the chest while taking a sip from his coffee.

They entered the alleged apartment with guns drawn, just in case the suspect was dumb enough to hang around. They cleared the living room with silent nods to each other as they bent every corner. The master bedroom was last, and Miller was first to enter. Grainger followed suit as they both froze in their tracks at the horror scene before them.

A naked female lay stretched across the bed on her back with a knife wound to her torso and another across her throat. Miller rushed toward her and checked for a pulse. He looked up at Grainger and nodded. "She's still alive. Get the paramedics in here quickly! And get somebody to pull the body up out of this fucking window!"

Miller commanded as he took off his jacket and surveyed the female's wounds. She was in a bad state, and from the looks of the scene, she had put up a fight, and was still combating for her life.

Grainger stood to the side as the paramedics entered the room and immediately started treating the woman. She was having trouble breathing, and her heartbeat was weakening by the second. They reached in their bags and started performing a tracheostomy to open her airway. Once she was breathing, but still unconscious, they put her on the gurney and wheeled her out of the room and down the hall.

Miller was looking over at Grainger, who was still taking everything in, and held up a bloody knife. "Looks like the weapon." He placed it in an evidence bag and used a pen tip from the nightstand to pluck the used condom from the floor. He looked at Grainger and shook his head. "Going off of a hunch, I'd have to say it was a rape/attempted murder/suicide," he said as he placed the soggy latex into another evidence bag. Grainger frowned his face up. He had read about them, but never actually had the chance to deal with a multiranged case in his career; either way, it wasn't their field.

Two cops finally pulled the body through the window and stretched it across the floor. Miller walked over and observed the man's stab wound and sighed. "She put up a hell of a fight," he said as he turned to Grainger. Grainger stepped around him and looked at the body for himself. He had to take a step back and sit on the edge of the bed to keep from collapsing. "You okay, youngin'?" Miller asked.

Grainger couldn't believe it. He had to stand up, take another glance, and flop back down on the bed. Within only weeks apart, he had responded to two of his old friends' murder scenes, well suicide/murder scenes. He didn't know what to think. The gravity of it all pulled at his heart and eyes with enormous force.

One rule as a detective: Never believe in coincidences.

"I'm good. I just . . . I just know him. We were friends in high school. Just like the other body at Cloverdale Park." Miller looked at Grainger, and then at the body. Grainger buried his face in his palms and took a deep sigh. "Aye, partner, I dunno why I'm saying this, or why I believe it, but these murders might be connected," he said as he looked up at Miller.

Miller shook his head and crossed his arms on his chest. "First of all, they're not. Second of all, this isn't a murder. This is a fucking suicide. The bastard obviously raped that poor girl," Miller said as he paused and pointed at the bag with the condom in it. "She put up a fight. They stabbed each other during the tussle." He pointed at the knife. "And once he overpowered her and got his rocks off, he felt guilty and rendered justice to himself." He pointed at the rope around Scott's neck as the officers pulled it off. "Whatever the case, it's not our case. Come on," Miller said as he walked past Grainger and signaled him to follow.

Grainger took one last look at his childhood friend and reluctantly left the room. Once they were in the hallway, they heard a commotion at the door with the officers who were guarding the scene. Grainger rushed forward to assist. A woman was throwing a fit as she pushed and shoved with all of her might to get past the officers. Tears streamed down her cheeks as she sobbed and shouted for permission to enter, but they just held her back and instructed her to clear the area.

"That's my fucking friend that you pulled out of there! What happened? Who's in charge here? I need answers!" she screamed as she tried to push through once again, but Officer Cherry blocked her path with a stiff arm to her shoulder.

The move was a little more forceful than needed, but then again, he was a rookie and didn't fully understand how to deal with those situations yet. Grainger stepped forward and stood in front of her.

"Ma'am, take a walk with me. I'll tell you whatever you need to know," he said as a ploy to get her away from the scene, as well as dig some information out of her.

"No, fuck that! Are you in charge? What happened to my girl! Is Scott okay?" She tried to peep down the hallway into the bedroom, but she couldn't see anything from her angle. Grainger placed a comforting hand on her shoulder and gently guided her back out of the door and down the hall.

"Man, is she . . . Is she okay? Be real with me . . ." Toni asked in between sniffles.

Grainger wrapped his arm around her. "We won't know till we get her to a hospital, but I'll be straight with you if you are the same with me. She wasn't looking good. She was stabbed and raped."

Toni stopped and faced Grainger with eyes of terror, hinted with disbelief. "That's bullshit! Scott wouldn't do that! Let me talk to him!" she bellowed as she turned toward the door. Grainger blocked her path and leaned over to speak to her.

"Scott committed suicide afterward. Hung himself out the window."

Grainger watched as her eyes nearly melted into pain's lava while tears erupted from her sockets.

"Did you know Scott well?"

"Well enough to know that he wouldn't rape my friend! Or kill himself! It's some fucked-up shit going on in there. I was just here! Everything was cool when I left," Toni said as she pounded her fist into her palm with each syllable.

Grainger looked at her, and then at the apartment door. He knew Scott back in the day, but not well enough lately to back up her character statement. Still, he was always a self-centered person, and his arrogant persona didn't match suicide.

"Listen, you head on over to hospital and be with your friend. I'll search around here for more clues to back up your story. I give you my word that I'm going to find out what really happened here tonight. That's my word," Grainger said a comforting word.

"Oh please! You ain't gon' do shit!" Toni said as she sucked her teeth and started to march away.

Grainger grabbed her shoulder and stood in front of her. "Listen, give me your contact info and I'll call you in the morning to clear some of this up. I promise you that I'm going to work this case. He was my friend also." Toni looked up at Grainger and rolled her eyes in disbelief. "No bullshit, Scott Zachary and I were cool in high school, and I'm with you on your theory. I don't think he was the type of person to do any of this."

Toni could detect the genuineness in the detective's voice as he spoke about an old friend. She believed him. She trusted him. She nodded her head and gave him a number to reach her by before they parted ways.

Grainger entered the apartment and met Miller standing in a corner sipping from a warm thermos of coffee. "Miller, that girl was here before this all happened. She doesn't think that he killed himself or raped the girl," Grainger started. Miller took a loud sip and smacked his lips.

"Well, the evidence proves otherwise, so fuck what she says," Miller said coldly.

"I don't believe it either."

"I don't give a fuck what you believe either. I hate to be blunt and nasty, but it's damn near midnight. I don't have time to play games with you, Grainger."

"Miller! That's another friend of mine that's in there dead! That's two in less than a month. Now something fucked up is happening. You have to notice that shit by now!" Grainger preached as he pointed down the hall.

Miller took another sip and glanced at his watch. "I'll tell you what I did notice. I noticed that you need to pick better friends," Miller said as he walked out of the apartment.

Grainger watched him as he headed down the hallway and entered the elevator. As the doors began to shut, Miller held his thermos up in a toast.

"To old friends."

Grainger walked through the department the following morning with his head held low. He didn't get a lick of sleep the night prior as heavy-footed thoughts tap-danced on the marble of his membrane. Seeing his friends slaughtered and zipped up in body bags made him fidgety and didn't sit well with him at all. Jontai's murder was typical in the lifestyle that he chose. That made sense in the fucked-up logic that justified it. Scott was a different story, however. Grainger still couldn't believe that he was capable of rape, and then taking his own life. Although he hadn't seen or heard from him in years, something just didn't feel right. He wouldn't believe it.

Grainger offered faint greetings to fellow officers as he made his way to his cubicle in the back of the room. He sat at his desk and waited for the computer to boot up as he leaned in his squeaky chair and folded his arms over his head. Finally, he opened the Internet browser and logged onto Facebook. He just needed to see something. None of his old crew was on his friend's list, of course, so he searched their names. He had no idea what he was looking for, but he'd know it if he saw it. Salem didn't exist. Brandon's page was private, so he moved on to Jontai's. Nothing was there but RIP pictures and messages on his wall from grievers. Grainger dropped his head and scolded himself for not attending the funeral. He honestly never gave it a thought.

He heard someone behind him so he quickly left Jontai's page and went back to his newsfeed.

"Tsk, tsk! Caught red-handed."

Grainger turned in his chair and faced Rollins with a scowl. Rollins leaned against the cubicle wall as he shook up a protein shake. The metal ball inside rattled against the plastic cup and annoyed Grainger more than Rollins's presence.

"Is this what we do now? Just play on Facebook as soon as we get to work? Man, I wish I had your career," Rollins said sarcastically.

Grainger watched as Rollins popped the top on his drink and devoured all of its contents right in front of him. "Is there something I can help you with? Or did you just come over here to ride my dick?"

Rollins closed the lid on his empty container as a drop slid down the corner of his mouth. He wiped it with his thumb and smeared it against the cloth of the cubicle wall.

"You're not going to say no, homo after that? Isn't that what's hot in the streets with you people?" Rollins asked with a grin.

Grainger shook his head and turned back around in his chair. He didn't have time or the drama-laced appetite to bite on the racist bait that Rollins was casting.

"Fuck outta here, Rollins," he said coldly.

"That's *Sergeant* Rollins to you," Rollins said as he started to walk away. A shout from across the room made him pause.

"Grainger!"

Grainger peeped up above his cubicle and saw Miller standing at the lieutenant's office door waving him over. "Get over here."

"Daddy's calling," Rollins taunted as he watched the look of annoyance spread across Grainger's face. Grainger started to walk over, but Rollins dug deeper. "Aye, word to the wise.

You better log out of Facebook before somebody posts a status about how you like to suck dick."

Grainger mugged him and turned back to his monitor. Before he logged off he saw the notification of a friend request. He closed the page and headed for the lieutenant's office. "Aye, Grainger," Rollins called out as he passed him. "No, homo."

As he made his way toward the office, Grainger pulled out his phone and tapped the Facebook app. He slowed his stride when he saw the name of the friend request that he had received.

Quinten Hazel

Grainger stepped inside the lieutenant's office and quickly shoved his phone into the pocket of his tan slacks. Miller sat off to the side on a small couch as he bit into an apple. Lieutenant Chris Cagle was fairly new to the department, but his presence was well felt. He was an ex-army drill sergeant and still sported the high fade even though he was balding in the middle of his pale scalp. He had small, beady eyes that gave chills as he hawked over his desk. Recently transferred from Maryland, it was written all over his face from day one that he was not thrilled to work in the small city, leading the homicide and narcotics departments.

Grainger met his stare as he waited to see the reason that he was summoned. He recognized that look from a superior too well. Grainger had seen it his entire career. "At the scene last night, I hear that there was a girl causing a bit of a ruckus," he started off as he crossed his arms.

Grainger shifted his eyes in thought until it dawned on him. "What happened to her?"

"I calmed her down and sent her on her way," Grainger answered. The loud crunch of Miller biting into his apple broke the awkward silence that followed the response.

"You sent her on her way? Did she say anything? Did you question her?" Cagle's voice rose with each question. "Did you even stop to think that maybe she was a fucking suspect?"

"No. I . . . uhh . . ." Grainger stumbled on his words.

"Let me explain something to you, Detective Grainger. I know that I'm new here, and we haven't been formally introduced, so let's do it now. I'm Lieutenant Cagle," he said as he pointed at his chest. "I'm not here to make friends. I'm not here to even make rank. I'm here to do my fucking job, and I expect those who work under me to do the same! Am I making my motives clear?"

"Crystal."

"Meaning, I don't have time for young, trigger-happy, Rambo-ass Hollywood cops!" Cagle said as he slammed his fist on the desk. "Yeah, that's right. I've read your file. I know exactly the type of shit bag you are." Miller broke out into a chuckle until Cagle's eyes met his. "Something funny?" Miller raised his hands in a sarcastic surrender. "Now, where's the girl? And please tell me why on God's green earth would you just let her leave the scene?"

"I let her go because she was extremely emotional, sir. I did get her contact information, and I was just about to call her in," Grainger half-lied.

"Oh, then by all means, give her a call," Cagle said as he sat at the edge of his desk and crossed his arms.

Grainger pulled out his phone and found where he had saved her number. He pressed Call and raised the phone to his ear as he glanced over at Miller. He waited for the phone to ring. Instead, to his disappointment, he heard the operator notify him that the number he dialed was not in service. The quiet room filled with the sound of Grainger's failure. He ended the call, looked at the number, and stuffed the phone back into his pocket with a sigh.

"Let me guess . . . wrong number?" Cagle asked rhetorically as he stood to his feet. Grainger opened his mouth to answer, but Cagle cut him off. "Shut it! Shut that fucking mouth right now! All I want you to do is go find that fucking girl!" he shouted as he pulled his chair out and flopped down.

He folded his hands in front of him like a praying mantis and massaged the bridge of his nose. "Detective Grainger, for the sake of what you consider a career, leave my office and go find that fucking girl," he said in a forced, calm tone.

Grainger nodded his head and exited the office, closing the door behind him. Cagle looked over at Miller, who shrugged his shoulders.

"You better get control of your partner, and I mean expeditiously. 'Cause if that Internal Affairs agent brings her sweet cheeks back down here, for any reason other than to give me some pussy, I'm going to kill you," Cagle said as he pointed across his desk at Miller. "I will cut your balls off and staple them to your fucking forehead for your open casket funeral." Cagle let out a deep sigh and closed the file in front of him as he moved it to the side and opened a different one. "Now, call Sergeant Rollins in here. I'm tired of his shit too."

Grainger stepped outside and pulled his phone from his pocket. He angled his back to block the sun's glare and opened the Facebook app. As he was about to accept Quinten's friend request, he noticed that he had a message from him, so he anxiously checked it. The message was short and to the point. Quinten had given Grainger his number and told him to call him ASAP.

He walked across the parking lot and dialed the number. As it rang, he shook his head at the thought that the woman from the scene the night prior had given him false information. He wondered what else she was lying about. Now the new lieutenant was all over him for answers to a test that he thought he passed a long time ago.

"Yo, Quinten? What's up, homie? How you living?" Grainger greeted when he heard the phone pick up.

"You know where the Italian Pizzeria is off of Sunset?" Quinten's tone was emotionless.

"Yeah, I've been there a few times," Grainger responded as he stood near his vehicle, confused.

"Meet me there in ten minutes," Quinten said as he ended the call.

Grainger stared at the phone for a few moments before sticking it back in his pocket and entering his vehicle. He hadn't spoken to Quinten since the latter years of high school and figured that they ended on a good note and sort of just grew out of each other, but Quinten was being real short with him, real cautious, and sounded real nervous.

***

The Italian Pizzeria was a small shop in Rock City that specialized in culinary arts painted with grease on thick dough canvases. The owner was a slick-talking, midthirties, Puerto Rican character from Brooklyn, named Kenny. He wore his oily hair low and tapered with a flawless chinstrap, resembling the '90s heartthrob R&B singer, Jon B. Although he moved to Rock City over a decade prior, his upstate persona was still thick and bubbled at his pores.

Grainger walked in and stood at the far end of the counter while Kenney dealt with a young male customer in a do-rag. Grainger used to come to the pizzeria a lot back in the day, but ever since he took a vow to fitness and a healthy lifestyle, he had sacrificed many of his favorite meals. Mainly because of his long-term girlfriend, Julissa. He smiled when he thought of the verbal thrashing she would give him when she saw the bank statement about where he was having lunch.

"Yo, Detective D., I'll be with you in a second. Let me handle this knucklehead right quick," Kenny said.

Okay, maybe Grainger did sneak to the pizzeria more often than not and had somehow become a regular, but Julissa didn't need to know that.

"Let me tell you something, youngin'," Kenny started. The male, probably in his early twenties, chuckled and crossed his arms.

"Nah! All I'm saying is that you are a band-wagoner," the young male accused. Kenny took a step back and frowned his face up as if he was deeply insulted.

"Listen to me, I'm from New York, a'ight? I was a die-hard New York Knicks fan, but that was back in the day. Feel me, like you are too young to remember, but back then, you were either a New Jersey Nets fan, or you were a Knicks fan. Me being from New York, naturally, I rooted for the Knicks, because that's just what it was. Now that we have the Nets, and I'm from Brooklyn, of course, I'm going to rep that shit, nah, mean!" The young male tried to interrupt, but Kenny held his palm out.

"Like picture this, if you will. You are from N.C., so you rep the Charlotte Bobcats, or the Hornets, or whatever the fuck they are now. But if Rock City was to get a team, let's call them the Rock City Fiends, right? Now, wouldn't you rep the Fiends?"

Kenny paused for a second and just as the guy was about to respond, he cut him off. "Exactly! So don't come at me with that bullshit. Matter of fact, Georgio, get this little nigga a kid's meal, a to-go cup, and a kinky straw," Kenny said to his assistant as he dismissed the young male and walked over to Grainger.

"My bad about that. What you need, fam? The usual?" Grainger smiled and nodded. "A'ight, one pepperoni calzone and a medium Dr. Pepper," Kenny said before he disappeared into the back. He came out minutes later and handed Grainger his order and rang him up.

Grainger sat at a small table near the window and waited for Quinten. Right on cue, a figure walked through the door and observed the restaurant. Grainger recognized his face and waved him over with a smile. It was good to see one of his old friends—alive this time. Quinten had finally gotten taller, but he was still scrawny as a broom and held on to his baby face. Grainger stood up and shook his hand before offering him a seat. It was a shame that they had allowed life to separate their friendship.

"Detective Grainger, look at you!" Quinten said as he nodded toward Grainger's button-up shirt that was neatly pressed, thanks to Julissa.

"What's up, man? It's been a minute."

"Right, it has. I'm good, though. How are you? Girlfriend, kids?"

"Nah, no kids, and I have a girl, but she lives in Greensboro. It's a weird situation."

"Oh trust, I know how it goes," Grainger said as he sipped his Dr. Pepper and nodded. "Why were you being so short and secretive on the phone? And, nigga, why did it take you this long to find my ass?" Grainger asked.

Quinten's smile faded as he glanced around and leaned closer. "All right, I didn't want to talk on the phone or Facebook, because I don't know who's listening, ya know?" Grainger wiped his mouth and leaned closer as well, hoping to hear some juicy gossip. "You heard about Jontai, right?" Grainger sat up straight and kind of smirked.

"Yeah, man, I work homicide. That's one of the cases that I'm working," he lied. He wasn't working it at all.

"All right, well, let me help you out. Here's a promising lead for you."

Grainger leaned back as he wondered if Quinten really had some credible information. He pulled a small notepad from his breast pocket and clicked his pen as he waited.

"Salem Knight."

Grainger looked up at him and stuck the pad back into his pocket as he shook his head.

"Seriously, Q? I thought you really had some-thing," Grainger said as he took it as a joke, but when he looked at the gravity of Quinten's brown eyes, he knew that he wasn't kidding.

"You for real? Mannn, stop. You've always been paranoid, and ever since that day, you could never get past that shit and just forget about it."

"That's the thing, though. Do you think *he* got past it? Do you think that *he* forgot about what we did to him that day?" Quinten asked as he leaned back in his seat. "I mean, look at Scott." Grainger lifted his eyes toward Quinten. It bothered him that he was saying everything that Grainger was trying to push to the back of his head. "Now, I've seen movies and read books. You detectives aren't allowed to believe in coincidences."

"Q, I get bodies every night. This is Rock City. Sadly, that's a norm here. Now, you are sitting there trying to tell me that all of them are related too?"

"No. Just the ones who played a part in what happened that day."

Grainger shook his head and took another sip of his Dr. Pepper, but Quinten's stare was merciless. "I think you're right. I think you've seen so many movies that you can't distinguish real life from *Final Destination*," Grainger said dismissively.

Quinten lowered his head and shook it. He looked up at Grainger and stood to his feet as he slid his chair back to the table.

"It was nice catching up with you. Hopefully, we can do this again . . . before it's too late," Quinten said as he walked over to the door. He paused and turned back to Grainger. "Dontarious, there was five of us involved, and two are already dead. That leaves, Brandon, myself, and you. We all know that if this is true, if my wild theory proves tangible, then he will save you for last. That leaves one question. Who is next?" Quinten waited for an answer that never came, and then nodded as he exited the restaurant.

Grainger stared at the door as the thoughts that he buried surfaced. He didn't want to believe it, but it was worth looking into. He knew that he couldn't bring the idea to Miller or the lieutenant, and his first task at hand was finding the girl. He had to know why she lied and disappeared. *What is she hiding?*

Red Rover

Brandon had left his old high school crew and purchased a new set of goons to strengthen his weak image. He was a coward, but his family had money, so it was easy to disguise himself as someone who had earned it. After high school, he no longer needed Jontai, and met a star athlete in college named Cedrick, who he kept at his side. The ladies loved Cedrick for his physique and his promising future. They loved Brandon for his lavish living conditions and generous gifts. Together, the two swept through the city of Greensboro, breaking hearts and jaws under Brandon's tyranny.

Cedrick never made it to the NFL, and to be honest, Brandon wasn't that upset about it. Now, he had a personal bodyguard to follow him into the real world. Brandon was selfish like that and only kept people around whom he could benefit from. If he shared his bread with you, there was surely a deeper reasoning behind it. It had been years since he had even thought about his high school friends. He couldn't care less where they were in life and had no desire to see them again. Their chapter in his book was finished, and he didn't have the time or space for an epilogue of rekindled flames.

Brandon, Cedrick, and Cedrick's younger cousin Tweek, pulled into Club Skyline's parking lot at a snail's pace. Cars were lined up behind them, leaning on their horns in impatience, but Brandon navigated the vehicle with grace. It wasn't that he was cautious, but he wanted to stunt. They were riding in his brand-new cherry-red Range Rover—courtesy of Mom and Dad as a late graduation gift. All eyes were on the luxurious automobile. Drug dealers in that area didn't even have that type of money, and Brandon loved the look of envy in their eyes. It was like he fed off of attention. If he didn't turn heads of admiration, it was like he was a rose in a dry vase, located in a dark corner of a room—he felt as if he would crinkle up and die. It was the love and jealousy that fed his wealthy roots.

He could've gone to any college in the world, but he chose Greensboro's A&T University, solely because he heard it was a party school, and full of average-class guys that couldn't pose a challenge to his inheritance. Brandon, the son of an x-ray tech and a lawyer, had it all, took it all, and didn't care whom he stepped on or left behind to keep his status.

"Yo, why you driving like this is a funeral procession?" Cedrick asked from the passenger seat. Unlike Brandon, he really wasn't a fan of the attention. He was from Greensboro and knew what it was like in the real world once you escaped the college district. That's exactly where they were; in the jungle. Brandon was spoiled to the power of his money and ignorant to the street code and how it couldn't be bought. Cedrick knew that the real goons were out, lurking. The real kings were in attendance, and they wouldn't take too kindly to some out-of-town lame trying to undermine their glory.

"That's because it is," Brandon said as he positioned himself lower in the seat and sped into a parking space near the door.

He hopped out of the vehicle with Cedrick and Tweek in tow. Tweek was only eighteen, but shared the same athletic build of his cousin Ced. Cedrick was keeping him under his wing, hoping to keep him out of trouble so that he could focus on college and pursue a career in basketball. Cedrick had failed in his own journey, but took it as his personal mission to make sure his cousin succeeded.

A bouncer in a tight black shirt that mirrored Cedrick's build and attire walked over and crossed his arms in front of Brandon. His dark shades and slick head made him fit the bill of the stereotypical door guard, but Brandon didn't seem fazed by his presence. He adjusted the sleeves on his Versace shirt, as if they needed it, and closed his hands together in front of him.

"Yo, that parking spot is reserved," the bouncer spoke in a deep tone. The vibration from the club shook the ground, but to Brandon, that was his presence.

"Yeah, I know. Thanks for reserving it for me," he said as he stepped past him and headed toward the door. The other bouncer stepped forward with a clipboard and immediately started flipping through the pages.

"Name?" he asked. He was hoping the arrogant youngster wasn't on the list, just so he could shut him down in front of the crowd.

"Brandon Lowe," Brandon said in a tone that suggested that everyone should already know who he was.

He felt like a star. He looked like a star. He drove a star's car, and kept the entourage of a star. It was time that everyone else in that city started respecting his social status. The bouncer slid his finger down the list and shook his head when saw the name. He looked up at Brandon who smirked, and then back down to the list.

"A'ight, let 'em in," the bouncer said over his shoulder.

He mugged Brandon and hated everything about the kid. He could smell it on him that he was a spoiled runt that never earned a dime in his life. Brandon recognized the glare and reached into his pocket, pulling out a twenty-dollar bill. He placed the bill on the clipboard and patted it a few times.

"Here. I know how hard that must've been for you," he said as he and his team made their way inside.

Club Skyline was packed, wall-to-wall, and Brandon loved it. Tweek was grinning so hard that his cheeks hurt. He was never granted access to clubs like that because of his age, so just walking through the door was an experience in itself. Cedrick wasn't too thrilled. He hated crowds, and he knew that being with Brandon in a place like that, with all of the hateful eyes that glared at them like goblins, it would only be a matter of time before something popped off.

Brandon walked toward the VIP section, located in the back of the club, and showed the bouncer his ID. Without hesitation, the rope was lifted and two bottles of Moët were

ushered toward the small table in front of the
two couches.

Brandon and his team sat in luxury as they
looked upon the sea of partygoers. The music
was high, the lights were low, and Cedrick's eyes
held at a medium squint looking for trouble.
Eventually, he relaxed and poured himself and
Tweek a drink.

"This nigga don't drink. Don't smoke. Don't
dance, but loves being in the club," Cedrick
announced to Tweek as he pointed at Brandon.

Brandon leaned closer so he could hear him
over the music. "I said, you don't drink or dance,
but love being on the party scene!" Cedrick
repeated over the floor-shaking bass. Brandon
nodded his head and smiled.

"Nigga, look around."

Cedrick and Tweek looked up and saw nothing but eyes focused on them and their section;
mainly a group of girls who weren't even being
discreet about their thirst. "You see that? Nigga,
I *am* the party," Brandon said as he patted
Cedrick on the back and reclined into the plush
couch.

Cedrick watched as Brandon made eye contact with one of the girls who was wearing a tight
purple dress that seemed stitched to her skin.

She smiled at him and bit down on her bottom lip. There was a perk to hanging with Brandon other than all of the free items of lavish. Girls loved that clown.

Brandon signaled the girl over, and she turned toward her friends. Tweek was watching it all play out and was getting excited. He wasn't an ugly dude and had experienced his share of females, but these women were older, and that fact alone held a higher plateau of exoticness. The girl in the purple turned back around and tugged at the bottom of her dress as if she cared about it rising and showing off her glossy thighs. She and her crew walked over to the ropes as the bouncer held it open for them to enter.

As they made their way toward the couches, Brandon got up and sat at the empty couch, signaling for the girl in the purple to join him. She complied, and her friends starting choosing between Cedrick and Tweek. Tweek tried his best to look cool and more mature, but it was obvious in the woman's lustful eyes that age held no merit with her. She was interested in something else. Her cleavage was singing songs of seduction as she sat beside him and rubbed her light hands over his jeans. Tweek had a weakness for redbones.

The girl in the purple didn't bother to sit beside Brandon. Instead, positioned her soft ass on his lap. She stared at him and rubbed her cheek against his like a cat in heat so he could get a whiff of her perfume. She could tell by the sparkle in his eyes that he was merely an insect becoming entangled in her web of lust—and the fact that his dick was poking the back of her thigh was an obvious clue as well.

"So what's your name?" Brandon asked.

He wasted no time and started kissing on her cheek and trailing to her neck. He didn't care who saw, and he knew that everyone was looking. To him, he had the sexiest chick in the club—an accolade reserved only for kings.

"I have a weird name, and sometimes I'm a bit hesitant to tell strangers," she said as she kissed him. She pulled back slowly as she sucked his bottom lip. She looked into his eyes when he finally opened them and knew that she had him right where she wanted him. "I was named after a variation of my father's name. People called him Tony."

The six members of VIP relaxed and chitchatted for the next hour. The bottles were nearly empty, with more coming in any moment, and the women were showing signs of intoxication.

Toni sipped her cup slowly as she eyed Brandon over the rim. It wasn't every night that she met a potential victim who had bottle service but didn't drink. Usually, she could use their inebriation against them, but that night she knew she'd have to be a bit craftier to reel in the big fish.

Just by looking at him and his relaxed demeanor, Toni could tell that Brandon was different than what she was used to. He was cocky but didn't say it. His clothes were flashy, but he wore the threads casually. His arms and chest sported no jewelry, and that wasn't common among ballers in Greensboro. Usually, she could spot her Moby Dick a nautical mile away.

The last few days for Toni had been rough. She took the trip to Rock City to see her long-term boyfriend, as well as a few other money pits that she frequented when local, but the visit went bad before it even started good. The new "client," as she liked to call her side flings, had committed suicide and nearly killed her friend in the process. She felt terrible about what happened to Neka, but her fear trumped her guilt when she was approached by the detective. The last thing Toni wanted was her name mixed up in an attempted murder case—plus, that would be one of the foulest ways for her main dude to find out about her infidelity.

That was the type of person that Toni was. When the kitchen became too hot, she would flee for fresh air. She ran from all of her problems and responsibilities in Rock City, and ended up hours away in Greensboro. The city was much bigger, and she could blend in with the heavy traffic of the nightlife. Rock City was small, and everybody knew everybody's business. Everybody.

"You good?" Brandon asked as he tapped Toni on the arm.

He noticed how she was staring down at the floor. She was deep in thought and for a moment she forgot where she was. All she could see were the paramedics rolling her friend out of that apartment building. She regretted ever leaving her.

"You faded?" Brandon asked.

Toni lifted her head and swiped her hair behind her ear to expose her smooth cheeks.

"I'm good, but you need to stop bullshitting and take a drink," she said as she grabbed the empty glass and filled it up halfway. Ignoring his objections, she handed him the glass and leaned into his ear. "If you get nice and loose, I promise I'll be naughty and tight later," she whispered as she glided her hand onto his lap and massaged his dick through the jeans.

She felt it throb and knew that she was making progress. Brandon put his lips to the glass and took a communion sip.

"Don't be a bitch with it." Toni taunted as she finished her drink and poured another.

Brandon wasn't about to let her grade him like that. In one swift motion, he finished the drink and slammed the glass onto the table as he pinched his eyes together to combat the burn.

Cedrick and Tweek nodded toward him as they stood to their feet holding their date's hand. Clutching bottles in each of their hands, Cedrick and Tweek led the women to the dance floor and disappeared into the crowd. "Let me guess, you don't dance either, huh?" Toni predicted.

"You guessed right. I just chill," Brandon responded as he tried not to frown his face up at the aftertaste of the beverage.

"I see that, but I like my man to liven up a little bit," Toni said as she poured him another drink, handed it to him, and climbed onto his lap again.

She positioned herself perfectly so that his dick was knocking on the door of her warm pussy through her thin dress. Brandon took another gulp of the drink as he stared at her cleavage that seemed to tumble out of her top.

The drink didn't burn as much that time, or maybe he was more focused on her riding his dick for real. Toni grinded against his crotch and moaned into his ear as she nibbled his earlobe. Right when the moment of lust was heated up inside the stuffy building, one of the workers walked over holding a bottle of Luc Belaire Rosé. She tapped Brandon on the shoulder to get his attention as she smiled with big brown eyes and pink eye shadow.

"Compliments of the gentleman over there," she said as she handed the bottle to Brandon, but Toni accepted it and examined the label in thirst.

Brandon looked in the direction that the girl pointed and saw a figure with long dreads and dark shades tilt his head toward their direction and raise his glass with a smile. Brandon automatically didn't like the obvious hoodlum who was trying to stunt on him by buying him a bottle. That may or may not have been the guy's intentions, but that was how Brandon took it, and he refused to look like a lame in front of his new meat.

Toni thanked the girl and was reaching for her glass when Brandon grabbed her wrist with gentle force. "Nah, send that back to him," Brandon said. The girl and Toni looked at him confused.

"Tell that nigga I got my own money. He can keep his," Brandon said as he waved the girl away and leaned back into the sofa.

Toni was turned on by his exhibit of power and could feel her pussy tremble just a little. She planted her lips on his neck and made her tongue paint his skin. Brandon wanted to close his eyes and enjoy the moment, but he watched over Toni's shoulder as the girl walked back to the bar where the man was standing. She handed the bottle back to him and whispered something into his ear. He looked toward Brandon, rubbed his face, and shook his head before storming away into the crowd.

Brandon smiled at his stunt. There was no way some hood nigga was going to try to carry him. Toni's tongue felt good on his skin. He had enough money to buy the club and charge fuck niggas extra just to parking-lot-pimp. Just as he was standing at the podium in his mind ranting about crabs in a poverty barrel, he heard two gunshots crack the air.

Both of their heads turned toward the dance floor as the crowd took off into mayhem, headed for the door. Toni jumped to her feet, and Brandon slid to the edge of the couch trying to get a better feel of what was going on. Two more shots filled the air, and the crowd dispersed like roaches in a sink. In the middle of the now-empty dance floor Brandon saw the bodies of Cedrick and Tweek, disposed like garbage.

It took a moment for reality to kick into his brain and send orders to his feet, but Brandon hopped up, shoved Toni out of the way as she fell over the table with the empty bottles, and he dashed for the nearest exit. He had no idea what or whom he was running from, but the image that was pasted on the back of his eyelids was a bloody portrait of his friends lying lifeless on the floor. All he knew was that he didn't want to lie with them, so being true to himself, he ran.

Finally he made it out the door with the crowd as they resembled a swarm of bees leaving the hive. Without skipping a beat, Brandon dashed toward his truck and climbed inside. His mind went blank momentarily, as he forgot how to start it, but every time he looked out the front window, every guy that ran by looked like a killer. Brandon started the truck and threw it into reverse. He didn't give a fuck if any pedestrians were behind him, but he turned to glance anyway—and when he did, he saw a figure sitting in his backseat. He nearly jumped through the sunroof as he stomped the brakes and hit the dome light. He was halfway thinking/hoping that the bodies he saw on the floor weren't his team, and one of them was in the backseat, but the light proved him wrong.

The figure smiled and leaned forward as his dreads swung off his shoulders. It was the same guy who tried to buy him the bottle inside. Brandon was frozen as a thousand questions flooded his brain and paralyzed him.

"You wouldn't leave a friend behind to die, now, would you?" the figure spoke.

He took off his shades and snatched the dreaded wig from his scalp, exposing a bald head and a familiar face. "Of course you would," Salem said as he shoved the barrel of a pistol into Brandon's side. "Let's take a drive."

Brandon was shocked, to say the least, and very confused. He had a gun pointed at his ribs, and an old childhood memory that he thought he had buried years ago had come to surface. For the sake of his life, he did what he was told and navigated through the chaotic parking lot. People didn't even notice his expensive ride anymore as they were too focused on reaching their own. For the first time in his life, Brandon needed attention . . . He needed someone to look at him and save him from his fate, but he went unnoticed.

He pulled onto the street and made a left as other cars turned right toward the city. A flock of cop cars with their sirens blaring passed by him, and Salem jammed the weapon deeper into his side as a reminder.

"Where are we going?" Brandon found the courage to ask. He glanced up at the rearview mirror, more like a cabdriver than a hostage.

"Take the back roads toward the hospital," Salem said. "Man, this is a nice vehicle!" Salem patted the caramel leather seats. "Another gift from Mommy and Daddy, I bet."

"Why are we going to the hospital?" Brandon asked in confusion.

The few drinks that he had were starting to blur his eyes, so he blinked heavy in attempts to clear his vision. The back roads were dark and desolate and never traveled during that time of night.

"Because you've been shot," Salem said as he aimed the pistol at Brandon's thigh.

As Brandon looked up into the mirror he saw the flash and felt the pain rip through his flesh. It felt like someone was holding a welder's torch to his skin. He screamed in agony and swerved across the road.

"Settle down, settle down. Pay attention to the road," Salem said as he grabbed the wheel and corrected the vehicle. Brandon slammed on the brakes, sending his own skull crashing into the well-padded steering that absorbed most of the force. "Good thing you went with the leather option, huh?" Salem joked. He grabbed Brandon by the collar and snatched his body backward. Brandon was grunting and sucking spit through his teeth as tears cluttered in his sockets.

"Are you fucking crazy?" Brandon mumbled.

The Range Rover was now stopped in the middle of the road, surrounded by trees and only the noise of the engine and Brandon's pains.

"Calm down and drive. You made me climb that house after you shot me. Man up," Salem reminded him.

"The fuck do you want from me?" Brandon shouted. The pistol returned, except this time the hot barrel rested on his temple.

"Just drive," Salem said. Once his point was made, he sat back in the shadows.

Brandon shook his head in bewilderment as he stared at the quarter-sized hole in his jeans. Blood bubbles were forming and leaking into the seat. He wondered why Salem didn't just kill him there. They were out in the middle of nowhere. It was dark, and not even the moon was watching. What better place? Salem must've had a bigger plan.

He began to drive, still holding on to the hope of an oncoming car. He had to drive with his left leg now and with all of the pain echoing through his body, this maneuver proved difficult as he had to let off the gas and constantly adjust his position.

"Are you going to kill me?" Brandon asked in a nonchalant tone.

The pain was excruciating, as his thigh felt like it was on fire and blistering frigid at the same time. The wave of irony hit him, because he was injured in the same spot that he had shot Salem years prior.

"No. Your actions will," Salem answered.

He was still relaxing in the shadow of the backseat. His eyes were fixed out of the window, taking in the scenery of passing trees and drooping power lines. He seemed more like a subtle passenger deep in thought than someone who was holding a hostage at gunpoint.

Brandon prayed silently for traffic to come heading his way, but God was silent this dark night. On that forsaken road, it was just him, Salem, and a quiet bitch named Karma.

Panic hit, or maybe it was heroic stupidity. Brandon knew Salem was going to kill him and made his mind up that he wasn't just going to lie down and die. He tightened his grip on the wheel and glanced in the rearview mirror.

Salem was still looking out of the window with not a single care in the world.

"Well, motherfucker, I don't plan on dying alone tonight. I'll see you in hell!" Brandon screamed as he floored the gas pedal. The supercharged engine roared as they approached speeds well over eighty miles per hour.

Still, Salem sat in tranquility. He didn't even attempt to stop him.

"Stay dead this time, motherfucker!" Brandon shouted as he grinded his teeth.

"I've been hearing that a lot lately," Salem said as he slid into the seat belt.

Brandon closed his eyes and snatched the wheel toward a ditch and into the thick pit of trees. The truck flipped two and half rotations as the tires spun on air before landing on its roof in a loud clunk.

Car parts littered the scene like slum-dog villages. Broken glass littered the leafy grounds like New Year's Eve confetti. Engine coolant poured as smoke and the smell of burning rubber fogged the atmosphere. The vehicle was totaled, and fuel leaked back into the earth from which it came. Mother Earth would receive another child into her arms of eternity in due time.

Slowly Brandon's eyes opened. His vision was obstructed by blood and sharp shards of glass

that made it into his sockets, causing the simple
act of rotating his retinas a painful and nearly
impossible task. When his vision came to focus,
he was hoping to be in a hospital bed surrounded
by officers ready to take his statement about the
body in his backseat. Unfortunately, that wasn't
the scene that he woke to.

Instead, he saw stars filtered by branches of
nearby trees. He could smell the havoc he had
just created, as well as feel it in every inch of his
soul. The left side of his body felt useless and
numb compared to the wound in his right thigh
that still ached. His brain wasn't getting any
feedback from its signals.

He knew he had to move, either closer to the
road for assistance or deeper into the terrain
for safety. That was a deadly decision, because
if Salem somehow survived, he'd find him easily near the road, but there was a chance that
a Good Samaritan could find him as well. If
Brandon was to go deeper into the woods, Salem
couldn't possibly locate him in the pitch-black
surroundings, but neither could anyone else
before he bled out.

Brandon struggled to prop himself on his
functioning side. Observing his gloomy surroundings he saw the wreckage about fifty yards
from his position. The beautiful vehicle that his

parents spent a small fortune on was destroyed beyond recognition. There wasn't any coming back from that, but at least he was alive.

Brandon had a quick thought to scramble over to the car, locate his pistol, and put a finishing bullet into Salem's head, but that wouldn't complement his self-defense statement. Instead, he remained in his spot, waiting, wishing for a car to pass by and notice the scene. He had a quick vision of the car bursting into flames, Hollywood style, and roasting that son of a bitch that decided to pop in and ruin his night.

He glanced down at the wound in his thigh and wondered if it was still bleeding, but the thought of touching it sent chills through his spine. Speaking of spine, Brandon questioned if the left side of his body was paralyzed temporarily or permanently. The idea of being in a wheelchair for the rest of his life disgusted him, dehydrated his thirst for perfection, and cramped his style. He felt embarrassed and a bit vain as he pushed that thought out of his mind—he should've been cherishing those moments of peace, those moments of no Salem, and thanking the Lord that he was still kicking, even if it was only one side of his body.

Continuing his selfish thoughts, the image of his friends lying lifeless on the club floor shamed him. If only he had not left them and stayed on the scene he most likely wouldn't be in the situation he was in. But what-ifs and but-shits wouldn't help him survive now. He crawled in the shit storm that he was currently in and had no choice but to hold on tightly and wait for it to end . . . one way or another.

The sound of twigs breaking brought him back to reality. He scanned his surroundings the best he could with his stiff neck but saw nothing.

"That's the second time you have tried to kill me, Brandon."

The voice came from right above Brandon's propped head. The scene resembled a child being caught watching TV late at night as his pupils dilated and tried to comprehend what was happening.

"How did you . . ." Brandon stumbled with his words.

He tried to crawl away on his back and one usable elbow, but his efforts were hopeless. With every inch of progress he made Salem just stepped closer. Soon, Brandon was stopped by a mossy tree trunk, which he propped his back against it and faced the audible direction of his predator.

"What do you want from me?" Brandon asked in a faint tone. The vibration from his vocal cords hurt his chest to muster.

"I just want what you owe me." Salem squatted beside him.

"What do I owe you? You want money? I can get money. You know I can."

A glimmer of hope shot through Brandon's body. He knew that the universal language in this world was money, and his bank account was the Rosetta Stone.

"Your father's money is worthless to me—"

"Then what?" Brandon demanded as he brought his hand to his chest and scooted more upright.

"See, for the first time in your life, your parents can't save you. How does that feel . . . to be alone in the woods and certain to die?" Salem asked in a menacing manner.

The crickets of the woods chirped loudly, resembling Roman crowds in the Coliseum. Salem was holding Karma's sword over Brandon's treacherous heart, and not even a thumbs-up from the emperor of life himself could save him.

"Man, please . . . What can I give you? I'm sorry, man, I really am! We were just kids, for God's sake!" Brandon pleaded as spittle flew from his lips. He didn't want to die there—not there and not by the hands of Salem.

"My life back. The innocent li'l boy who chased rabbits through woods just like these. The goofy kid who only wanted acceptance. Can you give me *that?*" Salem inquired.

"You know I can't," Brandon said with tears mixing with the blood in his eyes.

"Then your life will do," Salem said as he gripped the top of Brandon's bruised head and cuffed his other hand under Brandon's defense-less chin. "Don't worry. You won't be alone much longer. You have a few friends waiting on you in hell." Brandon tried to remove Salem's hands but failed as his bloody grip slipped on Salem's cold skin.

"And a few more to come."

Snap!

Blind Man's Bluff

Grainger sat at his desk with his feet propped up in a chair as he flipped through the *Black Hawk* magazine. He knew that any moment the lieutenant would catch him lounging and chew him a new one for slacking on the case. The reality was, Grainger was assigned to find a strand of hay in a needle stack; the further he dug, the more his pride was punctured. There was no way he'd find that girl . . . the only witness to the massacre and who happened to give him the wrong number. She did that for a reason, because she didn't want to be found. Grainger didn't feel as if she was guilty of anything anyway. He could tell by the layered pain that clothed her eyes in sorrow—he'd seen that look before. His only hope at cracking the case was if Neka woke up from her coma.

Still, he had to do something. The theory was still out there. Salem was still out there, and if he was really on a rampage mission to kill off old friends, Grainger, browsing a tactical magazine, wasn't productive at all. That aside, Grainger still needed a new holster for his service weapon. His current one had a faulty locking mechanism. It wasn't a major issue, but Grainger made it one in his head as a defense to block the rushing thoughts of being sacked by Quinten's theory.

A head peeked over Grainger's cubicle and around walked Officer Cherry with a nervous yet excited look on his face. "Detective Grainger, is it a good time?" he asked as he motioned at the spare chair that Grainger was using as a footstool. Grainger nodded and sat up with the magazine face-down in his lap.

"What's up, Cherry?" Grainger asked as the officer sat down.

"Sorry to bother you, Detective, but, you know how it is as a new cop. There really aren't many role models to look up to, ya know?"

Grainger nodded. He was too familiar with the feeling of being a lost pup in the precinct. He could recall vividly how Miller and Rollins shunned him at the gate of his career.

"I was just wondering, like I know I'm new and a long ways away from any type of promotion, but is there something that I could be doing now to like, prepare myself for when that time comes? Like, to strengthen my résumé for when I do go up for the shield?"

"Well, keep your nose clean, for starters. I saw how you roughed up that witness at the last scene . . ." Cherry's eyes dropped in shame. "You can't do shit like that and expect to rise. One blemish in your file, and it will take a miracle to shine again. Show up early. Be the first one here, and the last to leave. Be the most motivated cop there is. Sign up for everything."

Grainger was just shooting shit now, but it felt good to be sought out for career advice. "Your colleagues are going to tease you and say that you are being an ass kisser, but that's what it takes to climb that ladder. There's always going to be an ass above you, and if kissing it is what it takes," Grainger shrugged, "pucker up, and show 'em how bad you really want it."

Cherry nodded and looked as if he was taking it all in. "That's some deep shit, Detective. Somebody told me that when I was in the army, but I was too young and hardheaded to take heed, ya know?"

"What was your job in the army?" Grainger asked. He wasn't really interested, but decided to make small talk.

"Oh, I was a vehicle operator. I drove convoys." Grainger nodded and diverted his attention to his vibrating phone. He looked at it and noticed that it was a text from Quinten.

"Yeah, it was real out there. You either kissed ass or never made rank, ya know?" Grainger nodded and opened the text. It was nothing but a link to a Greensboro telegram. "I should've stayed in and sucked it up, but I let my pride get in the way. Now I'm just here, looking for direction." Grainger waited for the article to load and glanced up at Cherry who was waiting for a response or something.

"Let me ask you this. Why do you want it so bad?" Grainger asked as his eyes bounced up and down from the phone to Cherry.

"Shiddd! I'm trying to make this money. Feed my family the legal way, ya know?" Cherry said. The look on Grainger's face let him know that he had answered incorrectly.

"You can feed your family working at Bojangles'. You don't do this job for the money. You do it for . . ." Grainger paused as he read over the article with silent movements of his lips. When he got to the end of it and saw that Brandon had mysteriously died in a car accident following a club shootout, Grainger slowly stood to his feet. "The fuck!" he said out loud.

"What's wrong, Detective? You were saying?" Cherry said as he stood beside him.

"You don't do it for the money. You do it for the legacy. Excuse me," Grainger said as he stepped past him and rushed into Lieutenant Cagle's office.

Cagle was sitting behind his desk with a pair of reading glasses dangling from his fingertips. Miller was sitting on the couch, and it looked as if they were discussing something important, but Grainger had a better story.

"Detective, you better be barging in here with a location on that witness," Cagle warned.

"No, but I have something even better. I have a theory." Miller rolled his eyes and sank deeper into the cushion. He knew what was coming next.

"Going over your files, Detective Grainger, I'm quite familiar with your theories. Spare me the bullshit," Cagle said as he put his glasses on and went back to reading the document in front of him. It was Grainger's cue to leave, but he wasn't ready to chalk it up that easily.

"His name is Salem Knight. He and I were friends up until high school, up until a group of friends and I shot him in the neck and left him for dead in an abandoned house." Cagle slowly raised his eyes and looked over the rim of his glasses. "Nobody had heard from him in years. Then all of a sudden, the people that were involved with that incident started getting killed.

First, Jontai Bridgers, then Scott Zachary, and now Brandon Lowe. They were all there that day, and there's only two of us left now. I feel that Salem is out there killing us off and that Neka was only collateral damage. His next target should be—" Cagle stopped him and raised his palm.

"I've heard enough," Cagle said as he went back to reading.

"I know it seems far-fetched, but I really bel—" Grainger pleaded.

"They said that you had an imagination on you, but damn! I'm actually impressed. Tell me, Grainger, have you ever considered writing books or something?"

"I'm serious, Lieutenant."

"And so the fuck am I!" Cagle said as he stood to his feet and leaned over on the desk. "I'm so serious about my job that I refuse to let you waste my fucking time with this bullshit! So somehow, after being shot, this guy comes back after all of these years, killing you all off? *That's* what you are standing there trying to feed me?"

"Yes sir. It's him. I'm sure of it." Grainger folded his hands in front of him. He knew he sounded crazy, but it was the truth.

"Listen, get the fuck out of my office and go do some real police work," Cagle said as he flopped down in his chair and sighed.

Grainger shook his head and turned to exit. He knew he was right and never really expected the lieutenant to believe him, but at least now he could say that he warned him. He needed to find Salem before he found Quinten.

"Grainger, find that fucking girl and stop reading comic books in your cubicle," Cagle shouted as Grainger closed the door. Miller looked at Cagle and shook his head. "You believe this shit? Salem? That's the fucking cat's name on *Sabrina, the Teenage Witch.* Jesus fucking Christ!"

Miller stood to his feet and walked over to Cagle's desk. "Lieutenant, I'll say this. Grainger's a fuckup, but there's one thing about him. When he has these hunches, they are usually somewhat true." Cagle couldn't believe what he was hearing, and Miller couldn't believe that he was saying it.

"So you believe that bullshit?"

"No, but it's worth looking into, or else we will look stupid again when he proves it right. I say we dig a little, make him feel like we are with him on this, and slowly nip it in the bud. Or else he won't rest until he finds this guy and stirs up a bunch of shit along the way. He's known to run off half-cocked when he gets focused on shit like this."

Miller had seen firsthand what Grainger was capable of when he was dead set on a belief. Cagle was still new to the station, so it was only normal that he had his doubts. Even for Grainger, this theory was a little out there, and Miller couldn't believe that he was even standing up for him.

"Okay—okay! Look into this Salem Knight guy and tell me what you find. When you come back with nothing, I'll shut this bullshit down and dare Grainger to go over my head with it." Cagle exhaled and rubbed his face in agitation. "Fucking guy is a pest! Nobody stays in more shit than that fucker! Nobody!"

Miller nodded and started to exit. He paused at the door and turned to Cagle. "It's probably nothing, Lieutenant, but just in case it is, we need to have our asses covered. I'll see what I can find."

Grainger stepped inside his dark home and tossed his coat and badge over the kitchen chair. The place was quiet—a little *too* quiet. Usually, Julissa would have the TV on in the living room, mainly because she was afraid of the dark on the low but would never admit it. He knew that she had to be home, and it wasn't late enough for her to be in bed, so his alert system immediately kicked on.

He carefully stepped across the living room and headed down the dark hall toward their master bedroom. With everything going on with the case, and the fact that he may be on a hit list that's getting shorter by the week, Grainger was getting extremely paranoid. He pressed his ear against the door and listened for movement inside. If Julissa was really inside and asleep that early, surely she'd be emitting that cute snore of hers that she forever denied. Grainger couldn't hear a thing, so he gave the knob a gentle twist, waited for the click, and then pushed open the door.

The bedsheets were pulled back neatly, almost invitingly, and that was rare for Julissa. Candlelight illuminated the environment with soft orange flickers that danced on dripping wax. Before Grainger could put the pieces together, a hand covered his eyes and mouth, causing him to nearly jump out of his skin. His heartbeat was looping at a high rate as the individual pushed him forward toward the bed.

As he fumbled for his balance, Grainger heard the speakers turn on, and Julissa's favorite song by J. Holiday, "Bed," started playing through the Bose system. He looked up and saw his chocolate goddess standing in the doorway. She had changed into that Victoria's Secret thing that he liked.

There was no getting out of this one. Grainger smiled and knew what was coming next. Lately, he had been swamped at work and letting the pressure from the job have a negative effect on his love life. Not this time, though. Julissa needed some attention, and that night, she had his undivided. Her perfume sprayed there, his favorite fragrance of hers . . . Love Is in the Air.

She seemed to glide across the floor. Her body reflected the candlelight, raising the temperature in the room. She pushed him onto the bed and tossed her leg across his lap as she straddled him and began unbuttoning his shirt. She tossed it on the floor and yanked his tank top over his head as well. Her soft palms rubbed his back.

"Uh-huh," he said as she touched him like she cared.

She stared into his tired eyes and just wanted to repay him for the week that he'd been through. She knew her man was under a lot of pressure, even though he rarely expressed it. He was focused now though. He wrapped his arms around her and unhooked her bra, exposing her perfect breasts and igniting the furnace in his pants. She stood up and wiggled out of her black-lace panties and started to twirl them on her fingertips like an amateur stripper.

Grainger snatched his remaining clothes off like a bench rider who was finally getting in the game. His dick stood erect and throbbed at her every movement as she grabbed his shoulders and hovered over his rock-hard shaft. She slid down it with ease as her juices leaked around her southern lips, going lower and lower until he was fully inside her. Then she let out a soft moan and slowly started riding her man, sending their bodies into a merry-go-round of ecstasy.

He rubbed his fingers through her hair as he was wrapped up in her legs. Her eyes started to roll back, and both collapsed onto the bed. Her motion went from slow and passionate to fast and erotic as her cheeks bounced on his thighs. She licked his neck in the spot that he liked and trailed her tongue upward till it met his. Her soft lips sucked on his tongue as her pussy lips clenched and tried to suck the nut out of his dick. Grainger wasn't ready to come yet, so he turned her over. Love was war, and he was her soldier.

He delivered long, slow strokes, removing his dick all the way out of her before jamming it back in and completing a circular motion. Julissa tried to use her palms in his chest to shorten his thrust, but Grainger wasn't having that. She had begged all week for some dick, and she was about to take it all.

He grabbed her hands and pinned her down with her legs on his shoulders. She nearly screamed when he went as far as he could inside her vulnerable walls, breaking through every defense mechanism she tried. He wanted to make her remember that fuck, just in case it was their last one. The rage built up inside him as he started pounding like a porn star in a finishing scene. She was so open you could hear his dick pushing air out of her pussy, muffled by the sound of their skin clapping against each other.

He flipped her over and didn't even give her a chance to get to her knees before he reentered her as she lay on her stomach, trying to catch her breath. He mounted her like a boogie board and surfed her flooded walls, sending tides of orgasms through the sea of her rippling flesh. He could feel himself about to nut, so he grabbed her hair, pulled her face toward his, and delivered his prestige as he kissed her passionately. Sweat lubricated their bodies, easing the friction as Grainger's cheeks clenched, and he exploded deep inside the love of his life.

He tried to pull out afterward, but she arched her ass up and bounced on his sensitive tip more. Grainger pulled out and stood to his feet as their eyes met, both exhausted, sweaty, and leaking from their love-makers.

"You better be careful who you sneak up on," Grainger said faintly as he caught his breath.

Julissa just stared at him. That was exactly what she needed, and she would definitely go for round two, but first, she just wanted to rest her eyes.

Grainger smiled when he noticed that she had passed out and was already snoring; it boosted his ego as he walked over to turn the music off. "I'ma put you to bed . . . ed . . . ed . . ." he sang quietly in celebration.

As he turned the music off, almost as if they were synced, his phone started ringing. He found it in his pants and answered it.

"Detective Grainger?" the caller asked.

"This is he," Grainger answered as he sat on the cold, damp sheets.

"Yes sir, sorry to bother you this time of night, but this is Dr. Wellcher here at Nash General Hospital." Grainger stood to his feet, expecting the worst. "You told me to call you when Neka Harrison was awake from the coma."

"Yeah, yeah. I remember," Grainger said, as his heart seemed to stop. Everything in the world got quiet as he waited for the doctor's next words.

"Well, she's up."

Grainger made his way down the hospital hall, taking anxious steps, paying attention to the numbers on the room doors. He needed Neka to verify his theory. She was his only hope he had at possibly saving lives, saving *his* life, at that.

Salem was always a weird psychotic kid, and now he had matured from torturing animals to hanging victims out of apartment windows—all of this over something that happen fourteen years ago. He had to admit it sounded crazy when he pitched his theory to Lieutenant Cagle, and he never actually expected them to believe him. He just needed to say it out loud and have someone confirm how outlandish the idea was that danced in his head. Either way, no matter if he or Miller believed it, the evidence was apparent. Salem was mentally fucked-up. He left a witness alive, and Grainger planned on capitalizing on that flaw.

Grainger hated hospitals. There was something about the smell of latex and the cold temperature that instigated chill bumps on his neck, along with the beeping of machines, the random voices of laughter, and cries. It all spooked him. The hospital was where life began and life ended: the gateway, the checkpoint of existence, and here was Grainger, speed walking toward the room of a recovering victim to gather information. Was it for the case or for his own personal security? Grainger couldn't answer that. He didn't want to admit that he was scared, so he hid behind the badge.

"Hi," Grainger said as he peeked in the room.

Neka's mother was at her bedside, smiling at her with a face that was soaked with the mixture of joyous tears and sympathy. In the mother's arms was Neka's son, sleeping peacefully, oblivious to what was happening around him. They both turned toward the door when Grainger spoke. He held his badge in the air and hid behind it. The mother motioned for him to come in as she stood to her feet and met him in the center of the room.

"I know you have a job to do, but please make it quick. My baby has been through enough, and I'm not sure if she is quite ready to relive that night just yet." The mother switched the arm she was holding the child in and leaned closer to Grainger in a whisper. "But I want . . . I *need* . . . you to catch this son of a bitch. So please, go get whatever information you can from her and bring forth due justice," she said as she patted his shoulder and left the room.

Grainger walked over to Neka's bedside and smiled at her. He never expected her to survive, especially after how she was found, but somehow she pulled through.

"Neka, how are you doing?"

"I . . . I'm okay . . ." she struggled to say.

Her voice was crackly and distorted, but she tried to sit up and seemed as if she'd cooperate.

"I know this is a bad time, but we really have to catch this guy, you understand?" Neka nodded and cleared her throat. "Did you see who did this to you?" She nodded. "Did you recognize him?" She nodded again. "Can you give me a description of what he looked like maybe?" She took her hand and waved it over her face. Grainger frowned, trying to decipher what she was trying to say.

"It was dark. Happened too fast." Grainger had a look of disappointment on his face. "It was the same guy that—" Neka broke into a series of coughs and held the bandage on her neck. Her mother looked through the blinds to make sure everything was okay, and then went back to pacing in the hallway.

"Take your time, Neka," Grainger instructed as he squatted near her bed.

"It was the same guy that that showed up to my house the night Jontai was killed."

Grainger stood to his feet and rubbed his face. He had a feeling he was right, but hearing it authenticated out loud was different.

"Are you sure about this? How do you know if you never got a good look at him?" Grainger asked.

He believed her, but he needed to ask the questions that he knew Lieutenant Cagle and Miller would ask him when he brought this evidence to them.

"Trust me, I remember the way he smelled, like . . . aloe or something. That cold look in his eyes. The way he spoke in riddles, and his fuck . . . his fucking voice. I'll never forget that. It was him, I'm sure of it."

Grainger had all he needed for the time being. He placed a hand on her shoulder and smiled at her.

"Neka, you've been very helpful, and I vow to you that I will catch this guy. You're a strong woman to survive what you went through. Get some rest, and I'll come back later with more questions. Okay?"

Neka nodded and turned her head as tears started to roll down her cheeks. As Grainger exited the room, he nodded at her mother and disappeared down the hallway. It was official.

Rock City had a serial killer, and Grainger happened to know him personally—an old best friend, with childish grudges. All Grainger had to do now was find him.

Neka blinked her eyes open and saw a doctor entering her room. She had endured a rough night, but all in all, she was happy to be alive. She sent her mother home to get some rest. After sleeping on the hospital recliner for weeks, she knew that her mother missed her bed terribly. Her mother resisted, but eventually honored her request. Neka just needed a night alone to cycle her thoughts and piece together what was left of her life.

Now it was nearly midnight, and some doctor was in her room, disturbing her, flipping through pages on a clipboard as he stood in front of her bed.

"Neka Harrison?" he said as if he wasn't sure which patient he was visiting. He must've had a long night as well.

"How are you feeling, ma'am?" Neka nodded her head as he stepped to the side of her bed and placed the clipboard on the chair. "I know it's late, and I hate to disturb you, but we need to give you a little happy juice to help combat any potential infections. Your body is weak after the trial that it's been through, so this is very essential. Okay?"

"A needle?" Neka asked faintly.

"I'm afraid so. I understand your fear, though," the doctor said.

After being sliced open like a pig at a black family reunion, it was normal for anyone to be afraid of sharp objects. Lucky for her, he was a professional and knew just how to sell his technique.

"I tell you what, just close your eyes," he said as he held her wrist. His touch was cold through the latex glove against her warm skin. "All you will feel is a slight pinch; then everything will be all right. Okay?"

Neka nodded and closed her eyes. She was waiting for the pain to come, but if a short pinch of pain would ease the aches that swarmed her body, it was totally worth it. She took a deep breath and held it; then her senses kicked on. Through her nose, she caught the familiar smell of . . . aloe. When she snapped her eyes open, the doctor covered her mouth with his rubber glove, and yanked on a plastic tie that locked her left wrist to the bed railing.

Neka tried to scream when she recognized what was going on, but he squeezed on her jaw with enough force to almost break it.

"You were never part of the plan, Neka," Salem said in a low, stoic tone. He held up a short scalpel and placed the cold steel against her cheek. "You just happen to always be at the wrong place, at the wrong time, around the wrong people."

Neka's eyes watered like morning sprinklers as she looked her killer in his pupils. Salem took the blade and sliced her wrist. Blood shot everywhere once her vein was severed. He smiled, and then cut the plastic tie, freeing her arm. He then placed the scalpel on her chest and stood back as she reached for him with her damaged arm, flinging blood across the room like an abstract painter. Salem's plan was a masterpiece. She could tell he was smiling through the doctor's mask as he folded his arms.

"I'm sorry, Neka. Maybe one day, at the gates of hell, you will find it in yourself to forgive me."

Neka grabbed the scalpel with her right arm and swung at him to no avail. She wanted to scream, but she could feel her body getting weaker by the second and sinking into the bed. Her deathbed. The sight of all of her blood made her queasy. Her blinks became slower and slower, and eventually her eyes never reopened. Salem smiled at his work and leaned in closer to her face as she still held the scalpel in her hand.

"Because suicide is a sin."

Salem walked back out, just as he had come, and paused at the door. He turned and looked at Neka's lifeless body once again and shook his head. "Oh, Dontarious . . . The things we do for friendship . . ."

Duck, Duck, Ghost

Grainger stormed in Lieutenant Cagle's office the next morning with a smile stretched across his exhausted face. Miller was sitting in his normal position, sipping from his thermos with his legs crossed. Grainger approached Cagle's desk and leaned on it as Cagle folded his arms over his head.

"I got it. I have living proof now, Lieutenant," Grainger said in an ecstatic tone, resembling one of a child announcing to his father that he made the basketball team.

"Oh yeah? Do tell," Cagle nodded for him to continue with a straight face. Miller shook his head and took a loud sip.

"Neka woke up last night. You know, the girl we found at the second scene. The supposed rape victim and only survivor of this sicko."

"Is that right? The only survivor, huh? And what did this survivor have to say?"

"Well, first, I spoke to the nurse. She confirmed that Neka wasn't raped," Grainger smiled, but

Cagle held his poker face. "That's not Salem's MO anyway."

"And tell me again, Detective Grainger, what *is* his MO?" Cagle asked as he leaned forward.

"To fuck me over and eventually kill me." Grainger stepped back and rubbed his head. He was feeling jittery and anxious to prove his case. He'd finally found the lead that he needed to prove his theory. "She confirmed that the same guy she saw at the second scene was the same guy that came to her house and asked about Jontai Bridgers on the night that he was murdered. I'm telling you, Lieutenant, it's real! And this guy won't quit until everyone that was involved that day is dead."

An awkward silence swept through the room as Cagle stared at Grainger with judgmental eyes. "Still don't believe me, huh? That's okay. I'm headed back over there to get an official statement from her." Grainger smiled and grabbed the doorknob, but Miller's words stalled him.

"Good luck with that. They moved her room," Miller said.

"Okay. What does that matter?" Grainger shrugged.

"She's now located in the morgue," Miller answered and raised his cup to his lips.

"The morgue? She died? You're fucking bull-shitting me! I was just there! I spoke to her!" Grainger snapped. He observed their faces to see if they were fucking with him, but their cheeks only held a sinister smug for watching him fail again.

"That may be the case, but she's dead now, so . . ." Cagle said nonchalantly.

"Fuck!" Grainger said as he started pacing. "How? I bet Salem snuck in and killed her! I'm sure of it!"

"Nope. She killed herself." Miller answered.

"Suicide? Fuck no! Who survives all of that, and then kills their self?" Grainger held his arms out, open for a response.

"Someone who doesn't want to live with the scars," Cagle said.

Grainger looked at him and shook his head. He couldn't believe what was happening. It just couldn't be possible.

"Heads-up," Miller said as he stood up and pointed out the door.

Neka's mother stormed in the precinct with tears and a face of rage. Grainger stepped out of the office, and she made a dash right for him.

He stood there as she grabbed his collar and shoved him against the wall with tears and spit-tle flying from her face. "*You* did this! It was you!

You fucking scum!" Grainger held his palms up and wanted to plead with her, but there was nothing you could say to a mother in that position. She had been through hell over her daughter, only to meet despair after a glimpse of hope.

"What did you say to her? What the fuck did you say to make my child do that? Tell me!" Grainger opened his mouth, but his words were too afraid to leave his lips, like first-time skydivers panicking at the door.

"Why?"

Officer Cherry rushed over and tried to pull her away from Grainger, but she wasn't holding on to just his collar, she was holding on to the last memory of her child. "Why did you take my baby away from me? Just . . . Please tell me, why did this happen to my baby?" She calmed her voice and broke out into deep sobs as she finally let go and buried her face into Officer Cherry's chest as he escorted her out.

Grainger stood there. His knees became weak and gave out as he slowly slid down the wall with murky eyes of salty tears. He had failed, and everyone was now looking at him as a failure. A once-hero of the Rock City Police Department, now a villain. An outcast. That's exactly what Salem wanted. He wanted Grainger to feel his pain—at all and any expense.

Grainger covered his face with his hands as tears leaked between his fingertips and traced the veins of his knuckles. He was destroyed. He was lost. He was alone in the woods and just wanted to die.

"Fucking Salem," he mumbled with shaky lips. "I thought there were rules to this sick game of yours. Why her? Why?"

Miller helped Grainger to his feet and escorted him back into Cagle's office. Grainger took a seat on the couch and fixed his face as he tried to avoid eye contact, but Cagle and Miller were staring a hole in him.

"What? You want me to say I was wrong? Fuck that. I still believe my theory. That girl was alive when I left, unbothered, and ecstatic to see the tomorrow that she was promised. That fucking Sa—" Grainger leaned forward and rubbed his temples out of frustration. "Salem killed her and made it look like a suicide. I fucking guarantee it."

"Grainger, we wanna believe you, but like you said, that doesn't match his MO," Miller spoke up as he leaned against Cagle's desk. "It doesn't fit his criminal profile."

"What criminal profile? He's a psychopath. He obviously doesn't play by the rules."

"That criminal profile," Cagle said as he pointed at the door.

An older white gentleman from the intelligence division walked in and laid a folder on Cagle's desk. He looked at Grainger for a second and dropped his head before leaving. Grainger was curious now. What was in that folder?

"You see, Grainger. I didn't want to give your bullshit any thought, but your partner here," Grainger looked up at Miller, "he said that it's worth looking into, so let's see." Grainger sat up on the edge of the cushion and said a silent prayer that there was something in that file to back his story up.

"Salem Knight, from Rock City, N.C. Lived with his parents, and then later moved in with his grandmother to finish high school in Bethel, N.C. He sustained a traumatic throat injury from a low-caliber rifle and underwent serious surgery at the age of fourteen." Cagle looked over the file at Grainger. "So far so good. He then failed tenth grade and enlisted in the military after completion of high school."

Bam!

"See, that's where he could've got his training. He was probably army infantry or some Special Ops shit," Grainger threw in with an excited tone.

"Calm down, hotshot. Says here he joined the air force and was a supply guy." Grainger lowered his head and shook it. "His career consisted of one deployment to Afghanistan, where he was attached to an army division in 2007, for thirteen months."

"There we go. He had to get trained by them. Right? Right?" Grainger opened the question up to the room.

"Possibly. They do have to train liaisons to meet the standards for the mission. We had some chair force guys with us once, shit bags," Cagle reflected, and then turned his attention back to the file.

"Well then, we have our background. I'm telling you it's him. As kids, he was always into that type of shit. Lieutenant, does it list an address for him now?" Grainger asked with a voice of hope.

"Sure does. Pineview Cemetery."

Grainger stood to his feet as his jaw dropped. Miller lowered his head and walked to the other side of the room. Cagle closed the file and folded his hands on top of it as he looked Grainger in his traumatized eyes.

"There ya have it. He was killed in action in 2008, a few days before his camp was supposed to come home. His tent was hit with an RPG one night, killing everyone inside. His body was sent home to his grandmother, who gave him a silent burial. And that, Detective Grainger, that's where his story ends. I'm sorry to hear about your friend."

Grainger couldn't believe it. It just couldn't be accurate, but he knew that Cagle wasn't the type to falsify documents just to close a case. He slowly walked toward the door as Miller held it open and turned around to face Cagle.

"Sir, he may have somebody doing it for him—"

"Are you fucking serious?" Cagle asked as his normal temperament began to boil again.

"Maybe a friend, carrying out his legacy. Maybe he told somebody about what happened. I'm telling you, sir, he has something to do with this. I promise you!"

"And I'm telling you, leave this the fuck alone. I'm beginning to question your sanity. Even if he had someone living out his last wishes to kill a group of guys who left him to die, why would they wait so long after his death? Huh? No answer, huh? Get the hell out of my office and focus on facts!"

Miller followed Grainger out of the office and grabbed his shoulder. "Listen, partner, don't get bent out of shape over this. We are all wrong sometimes. Nobody will think any less of you. You got that?"

"Miller," Grainger stepped closer, "take a ride with me."

Miller frowned his face up and had to take a step back. "After hearing that, you're still chasing this? Let it go, brother. Just let it go. I had your back on this because, honestly, I felt bad about leaving you alone during that last case. It was fucking with me, so I decided to give your theory a shot this time. But come on, Grainger. You have to know when to throw in the towel and come at this case from a different perspective."

"Just come with me, and if this leads to a dead end, then I'll let it go, like you say. I need you on this one, Miller."

Miller placed his hands on his hips and let out a deep sigh. He didn't want to tag along on another dummy mission, but if that was what it took to silence Grainger and his fantasies, then Miller had no choice.

"Okay, but if this shit turns out to be nothing, then you have to promise to leave this shit alone, and I mean it, Grainger," Miller said as he pointed his finger.

"Deal." Grainger was back smiling, and it was written in his pores that he had another plan.

"Where are we going?" Miller asked as he grabbed his coat from the rack and followed him toward the exit.

"Going to see Grandma Salem."

Grainger and Miller walked through the decaying lawn of the small brick home. Miller was hesitant, but wanted to go ahead and get it over with so he could return to his desk. He kept his eyes focused on the ground as he dodged random mud puddles and anthills. The residence had a gloomy appeal to it, with dying flowers leaning over cracked vases, weeds snaking up the siding, shingles peeling from the surface like sunburnt skin, and just an all-around old smell fogged the air.

Grainger knocked on the glass screen door and turned to look at Miller. A look of discontent was all over Miller's face as he brushed the debris from the hem of his slacks. A middle-aged white woman came to the door and for a second, Grainger wondered if he had the wrong home, or if Salem's grandmother had passed or retired to a rest home.

"Morning, ma'am. I'm Detective Grainger, and this is my partner Detective Miller," he said as he held his badge up to the glass. The lady leaned forward as if she was inspecting it. "We were just wondering if Mrs. Knight still lived here?"

The lady opened the door without saying a word and invited them in with a nod. Grainger stepped inside and immediately recognized the smell. Salem used to smell just like it. It was a mixture of soul food and medicine.

"Mrs. Knight is in the living room. I'm her nurse, so I must warn you if you are here to question her, she's suffering from early signs of dementia," the nurse said as she led them through the kitchen.

"Great," Miller mumbled.

The nurse pointed toward the living room where an elderly lady sat in a recliner with a blanket covering her lap. Her curly hair was gray and missing along the edges. The frames of her glasses were broken and rigged with tape but her lipstick, her plum red lipstick, was flawless.

Grainger walked in first as Miller stood at the threshold. The old western show *Gunsmoke* was on the floor-model TV as Mrs. Knight seemed deeply entertained by it in between sips of her coffee.

"Mrs. Knight?" Grainger said as he stepped in front of her.

"Baby, you are a handsome little shit, but I'm going to need for you to step out of the way of my show, ya hear?"

Miller chuckled as Grainger scooted to the side.

"Sorry about that. I'm Detective Gra—" he started as he kneeled beside her.

"Baby, I know who you are, Dontarious. You act like I didn't practically raise you and that knucklehead grandson of mines," she said as she raised the mug back up and stirred it with a spoon. This was hopeful. Surely if she remembered that, then her mind wasn't that far gone. "Baby, what time is it?"

"It's 10:32 a.m., Mrs. Knight," Grainger answered as he glanced at his watch. He adjusted his sleeve and decided to go straight into questioning. "That's kind of what we are here talk to you about. When was the last time you saw Salem?" Grainger asked carefully.

Miller looked at the mantle over the abandoned fireplace and saw a basic training graduation picture; that had to be Salem. The kid in the photo didn't look like he could harm a fly, let alone host a killing spree.

"Now, Dontarious, you know Salem died in, umm, what year was it? Anyway, he died, fighting that white man's war," she said firmly.

"I didn't know that, but let me ask you this . . . Have you seen him since then?"

Mrs. Knight's eyes shifted toward Grainger on his knees as the corner of her lips curled upward, and then released. "Child, I don't think you understand how death works . . ." she said as she stirred the coffee and took another sip.

"I do, but—"

"Baby, what time is it?" she interrupted.

Grainger lowered his head. He was getting nowhere, but he had a gut feeling that Salem was still alive. He had to have faked his death. That seemed like the only natural thing for a lunatic to do.

"Mrs. Knight, is Salem still alive? This is a very serious question, and innocent lives depend on it." Grainger had a little more aggression in his voice that time. Mrs. Knight set the cup down on the stool beside her and turned to face him.

"Only God determines who is innocent, child, and to answer your question, I buried my grandbaby years ago, in a cold grave, and I never got to see him again because of how he died." Her eyes faded off into the distance as she started rambling. "My poor grandbaby. His body burnt up so bad you couldn't even recognize him. That was the last time I saw Salem."

"Are you sure? Is there anything that you may be forgetting?" Grainger pushed. Miller observed the lady's face change and a flash of irritation blinked in her eyes.

"Thank you for your time, ma'am. My partner and I will be leaving now," Miller said.

Grainger gave him a look, but Miller's determined expression demanded that it was time to go. Miller disappeared into the kitchen and out the door as Grainger slowly stood to his feet. He gave the room a final glance and proceeded to exit.

"Dontarious . . ." Mrs. Knight spoke softly. "Sometimes we forget what we want to forget. It's just easier that way, right?" She reached down and grabbed her mug while cupping it in both hands. "That's just the way of life." Grainger stared at her and tried to decipher her riddle. "That way, fate comes as a surprise."

"What do you mean by that? What are you really saying, Mrs. Knight?" Grainger asked as he turned back toward her. He knew that she was holding something back. Maybe she felt more comfortable speaking to just him without Miller. "Tell me . . ."

"Baby," Mrs. Knight raised the mug to her mouth and slurped. She smacked her lips after she was done and smiled at Grainger. "What time is it?"

Two Truths and a Lie

Grainger sat nervously on the metal folding chair as he glanced at his surroundings. Funerals made him extremely uncomfortable—especially when certain beings pointed grieving fingers at him. He was the last one to speak to Neka alive—other than the killer. Grainger wondered if Salem even said anything to her, and if he did, what? Now Grainger was sitting at the grave site of another young lady that he failed. He failed to save her from a debt that he owed to Salem. Killing everyone that was involved that summer day in Cloverdale was one thing, but Neka was innocent. Salem had to be covering something up. Maybe he made a mistake.

Grainger looked at every face in attendance. Something didn't feel right, other than the obvious, and he had a hunch that Salem was somewhere nearby; somewhere smiling at Grainger, adoring his handiwork in the murder of a mother and beloved daughter, patting himself on the back with guilty arms tattooed in blood over the fact that everyone believed his suicide setup—everyone but Grainger, that is.

The layout was beautiful and themed with white roses at the base of the coffin which purified the visual of weeping eyes. Grainger shook his head. He could've avoided this. He could've stayed with her that night, had he known that Salem would stoop so low into the pitiless basement of cold-blooded murder.

Another regret that cycled through Grainger's head was the fact that he had left his firearm in his vehicle. He didn't truly expect Salem to show up and show out at the burial. After all, Quinten was rightfully next.

Toni and Quinten walked up late, mainly because she had to drive all the way from Greensboro on short notice. Quinten was happy to see the love of his life, but the occasion didn't warrant smiles. Still, he came to her best friend's funeral and provided a narrow shoulder for her to lean on. Even in all-black, damp eyes with slavering mascara, Toni was still the most beautiful woman that he had ever laid eyes on. He just wished that she was in town more.

Toni didn't tell him that she was actually there the night that Neka was assaulted. Of course, she couldn't; it would only incriminate her and give away her erotic past of infidelity. She loved Quinten, but she just felt that she met him at a bad time. A good man like him, with a stable job, didn't party. A God-fearing man head-over-Alaskan-hills for her was someone that she expected to meet later in life—later when she calmed her own life down. She wasn't ready to settle down just yet, but she also wasn't ready to lose Quinten, so she strung him along like a rescued puppy on a retractable leash. She also couldn't admit to being on the scene because she knew that the cops were probably looking for her for questioning.

Toni looked at the pearl-white casket and a part of her wanted to go see her friend one last time; another part of her knew that she wasn't strong enough to look Neka in her face after the role that she played in her demise. Toni felt 100 percent responsible. Had she not dragged her over to Scott's house for selfish pleasure, her friend would still be alive.

Toni lowered her head and pinned a tear back into her eye with her fingertip. Quinten wrapped his arm around her shoulders to console her, and she loved that about him. He had to know that she was fucking around, but it felt good to know that someone loved her no matter her flaws, no matter her involvement.

Toni looked up and saw a familiar face scanning the audience. It was the same cop that questioned her outside of Scott's house. Her heart revved up, and she took a step backward. Her heels dug into the loose soil, and it was as if the earth was trying to keep her in place to turn herself in, either to the authorities, or into the dirt where she rightfully belonged. He had to be looking for her, and if he spotted her he'd definitely question her—exposing all of her secrets to Quinten and a family of mourners.

"Are you okay, baby?" Quinten whispered in her ear as he placed a kiss on her cheek.

"No. I can't. I can't do this, Q," Toni lied. "Let's just go, please."

Quinten pulled her in closer to his chest in a warm embrace that she knew she didn't deserve. "You sure?"

"Yes, Q. Please take me back to your place. I can't stand to see my friend laid up like that."

Guilty tears slid down her cheeks, burning her skin, and threatening to peel the mask right off of her face and show the world who she really was. Her inner demon of lust, which, in turn, pushed her friend to suicide, was beginning to surface.

Neka wouldn't kill herself though. She was too proud of a mother. Her child alone was enough reason to convince her to live. Toni tried to dissuade herself from thinking more was involved in the situation. Even if there was, she didn't want anything to do with it or risk the chance of being seen by the killer or the cops at the burial. Quinten escorted her back to the car in silence as his arms seemed to protect her from all evil; well, at least block her face from being recognized.

"If I could, I'd like to say a quick word about forgiveness," the minister said as he stood in front of the casket.

He looked back Neka's lifeless body and shook his head slowly before focusing back on the audience. "The Bible talks about forgiveness. Forgive thy neighbor and the Lord shall forgive you. Don't go about your life holding grudges, hating someone or disliking them for something that happened years ago. Forgive, because that is the only way that one can truly be happy. You can't live your life with a smile on one side of your mouth and a frown on the other side. We as a people have to learn to forgive and let go—that's our problem."

The minister had Grainger's attention now, but his cell phone kept vibrating in his pocket.

He pulled it out and glanced at the screen. It was Miller, and probably about nothing important on a Sunday . . . probably only a reminder to show up early for a Monday meeting, so Grainger stuffed the phone back into his pocket.

"I want to speak to the family that lost this beautiful child. I know it's hard right now, and I'm not going to stand here and say that it will be easy. Forgiveness doesn't happen overnight, and due to the situation, it may be a hard pill to swallow, but you have to try. We all want to hate the person that forced this child to end her life but that's not God's way. Forgive! He will have to answer for his sins, so don't worry about that. Just open up your broken heart to forgive this cold world for allowing this to happen. Jesus can, and will, fix it."

Neka's mother turned in her seat and looked Grainger right in his eyes. She held her glare as Neka's son slept in her arms. Grainger took a stiff swallow wondering what would come next as she slowly opened her mouth and silently spoke to him.

"I forgive you."

Grainger couldn't do anything but lower his head. It was good that she found it in heart to forgive him, but he wasn't to blame.

His phone vibrated again and Grainger saw that he had a text from Miller. He opened it and nearly shouted when he read, "Get to the office now! We've got a lead on the killer." In a few swift steps, Grainger was back at his vehicle unlocking the door. He was so nervous that he couldn't get the key in and just yanked on the handle out of frustration, and it opened.

As he was stepping inside, he saw a car drive off, and the driver resembled Quinten. Grainger paused and wondered why he would be at the funeral, but he didn't have time to waste trying to draw a conclusion. He shook his head and hopped inside his car and pulled onto the pavement. His pistol was resting on the floor mat on the passenger side, and this pissed Grainger off. He was more careful than that, and his raggedy glove compartment was always falling open, spilling its contents on the floor.

He pulled away from the grave site with a smile on his face. He couldn't wait to see what Miller had found on Salem. He knew it had to be big if Miller's lazy ass was at work on a Sunday.

As he pulled onto the highway, Grainger saw Officer Cherry standing guard near the gates of the cemetery. Grainger nodded at him and was pleased that the precinct was finally taking the threat seriously, and the fact that Cherry had

taken his advice and volunteered for menial
tasks. Salem's days were numbered. He had
faked his death twice, and the third would be the
charm.

The department was chaotic. Everybody who
was somebody was running around, dropping
papers, and rushing into the conference room.
Grainger made it in just in time as Lieutenant
Cagle stepped up to the podium. Miller stood at
his side, and that kind of bothered Grainger; he
was the one who brought the case to light, and
there Miller was, soaking it all up like an iguana.
That was beside the point though. Grainger just
wanted Salem caught, or killed.

"Ladies and Gentlemen, let's bring it down
a notch," Cagle addressed the rowdy crowd of
anxious guns.

Nobody seemed to know what was going on,
only that it had to be something major to call
a Sunday morning briefing. Miller walked over
and manned the computer to control the slide
show.

"Sergeant Rollins, please close those blinds.
What is said in here today will stay in here, and
only circulate on a need to know basis. Got it?"

The crowd agreed with head nods. Grainger found himself, once again, sitting in the audience, attending a riddle that he should've known the answer to but didn't; the ritual in itself was depressing.

"So, thanks to Detective Grainger, we have been able to tie in a series of murders that track from Rock City to Greensboro." Heads turned toward Grainger and gave him a nod of approval.

Great, more light on a cop that they just witnessed crying on a wall.

"And with that, we have discovered an avalanche of bullshit, making this department look bad." Low voices spread among peers as everyone questioned what was going on. Even Grainger had to look around—he was lost now. "One of our own is suspected of these massacres, and I have officially issued a manhunt for the traitor." Grainger wondered if this was a trap. Did Salem succeed in framing him for the murders? Impossible. He was never that smart.

Cagle signaled Miller to click to the next slide and a photo appeared on the screen. The room got quiet as everyone stared and tried to make sense of the visual.

"Here is Officer Cherry," Cagle said as he turned toward the screen and pointed. "You may recognize him, because, yes, he was one of us."

Grainger opened his mouth to speak, but the next slide froze him.

On the screen was a group photo of an army infantry platoon in a deployed location. Cagle walked over and placed his finger on an individual in the back row of the portrait.

"Meet Staff Sergeant Timothy Cherry. This photo was taken in 2008 while he was in Afghanistan pulling a thirteen-month tour. I know a lot of you may be confused about why this is important, and I will enlighten you. This gentleman here," Cagle said as he pointed to a man standing beside Cherry, "this is Salem Knight. A documented trooper with mental issues, a violent background, and a personal vendetta against our beloved Detective Grainger."

Grainger couldn't believe what he was seeing, so he stood up and walked to the front of the room as he looked closer. It was Salem for sure, but why? Or perhaps, how?

"Are we sure that Cherry is the man?" Grainger asked.

Cagle nodded at him and walked back to the podium.

"Salem died during a base attack, but we have reason to believe that Cherry took it to heart and vowed to live out his legacy." Everything that was being said sounded far-fetched, even to Grainger. He just kept staring at the photo. It would explain why Cherry was so interested in him and always trying to get close to him, but it still was a gray theory.

"What reasons?" Grainger asked as he held his chin and stared at Salem's calloused mug.

It was almost as if the photo was speaking to Grainger, taunting him, warning him, and laughing at him and everyone in the room.

Cagle cleared his throat and took a sip from his water bottle. "We went off of a hunch. Officer Cherry was already in the eye of Internal Affairs for past discrepancies; then we found footage of him entering the hospital on the night that Neka Harrison allegedly committed suicide."

Grainger was still in shock. At least now Neka's mother could have some closure and stop blaming him, even though it wouldn't sit too well once she found out the true reason her daughter was taken away.

"Then, we acquired a search warrant for his home and found debris in his shed from a burned lab coat with blood on it. Forensics is still running the sample to confirm, but we are certain it was his disguise to murder the girl, and this is our guy."

"Why wasn't—" Grainger exhaled and rubbed his palm over his hair that was in desperate need of a cut.

He had been so stressed out lately over maintaining his sanity that he neglected maintaining his physical appearance. "Why wasn't I included in this investigation?"

Miller spun in his chair and answered for Cagle. "Because, if the theory was true, we couldn't risk you blowing it." Grainger faced him and raised a brow. "He was most likely keeping a close eye on you and the investigation. We had to throw him off by acting as if we weren't paying this situation any mind."

"Still, I mean, Lieutenant, this just doesn't sound right. Are you sure? I mean, I just saw Cherry."

The room got quiet, even quieter, to the point where you could hear the dying florescent lightbulb flickering. Cagle stepped down from the podium and stood in front of Grainger.

"Where? Where did you see Cherry? Nobody has seen him since this kicked off and we sacked his home."

"I literally *just* saw him working the detail at Neka's funeral," Grainger paused at the end of his comment and stared off into the distance. It was all making sense now.

Cagle looked over Grainger's shoulder at Miller. "There wasn't a scheduled security detail for that funeral," Cagle said as he signaled Miller to follow him and stormed out of the conference room. Grainger dashed out behind them as well. Even with all of the facts, it just didn't feel right. Cherry couldn't be the guy, and Salem was far from dead.

"Lieutenant," Grainger said as he ran in front of them and blocked their path, "this doesn't make sense. It can't be Cherry. It just has to be Salem. He's the only one who would go through all of this over something so petty."

Cagle poked Grainger in the chest and held his finger there. "Detective, Salem is dead, okay? Get that through your fucking head. Cherry is our guy, and all the facts are pointing at him."

"What if Salem is setting one of our own up? Have y'all even considered that?" Grainger asked as he spread his arms.

Cagle let out a deep sigh and looked at Miller who was shaking his head. "That's why we left you out of this. You are too emotionally attached to the case, and it's clouding your judgment," Miller spoke as he rubbed his graying goatee.

"I don't understand. You were all gung ho about us looking into this, and now you want us to fall back? This is *your* case, remember? You started this bullshit. You fingered trouble and got her all wet, and now that it's time to fuck her, you're pulling your pants up," Cagle said.

"Well, if this is, like you say, *my* case, then let *me* handle it," Grainger shouted as he punched his palm.

"Listen, Grainger, just step aside. This is above you now. You are officially removed from the case, do you understand? Stay out of it, and try not to get killed before we catch this fuck," Cagle said as he and Miller marched toward his office. Cagle turned to Miller and spoke in a low tone. "Keep an eye out for you know who. Once this shit hits the fan, I can promise you Internal Affairs will be all over the place."

Grainger just stood there, paralyzed in shock with his mouth stuck on stupid. Either Salem was the smartest killer alive, or Cherry really was their guy. It hurt him to admit it, but he was banking on the former. With all of the time, energy, and emotions that he had deposited into the case, he was now forced to withdraw.

Grainger stepped outside and pulled out his cell phone. He quickly found Quinten's contact and called him as he nervously tapped his foot on the cement steps. "Yo, Quinten, this is Dontarious. Listen, man, I believe you, bro, but I need you to do me a favor."

"And what's that?" Quinten asked.

"I need you to leave town, man. Salem is out here killing any and everybody that gets in his way. Maybe he will skip you if he can't find you.

We all know that I'm the main target. So can you do that for me, for you?" Grainger asked as he scanned the parking lot. There was no telling where Salem could be.

"Nah . . ." Quinten said coldly. Grainger had to look at the phone, baffled.

"What?"

"I'm not running anymore, Dontarious. I've made my peace with God, and I'm in a peaceful place right now. Whatever happens is God's will." Grainger flashed back to a conversation on a rooftop about God's will. "So if Salem wants me dead, he's going to have to go through God."

"Quinten, please, man, save yourself, bro. Get the hell out of here until this is over. We are real close to catching him. I'm talking *real close*."

"I'm closer to God—"

"Dammit, Quinten! Do you wanna live or make the fucking news, man? Stop being so stubborn. Leave town while you still have a fucking chance!" Grainger's temples were throbbing at how foolish Quinten was acting. He knew he was a very religious person, but at some point, you have to stop waiting on God to react, and be proactive. "Man, do it for me. Just leave. The rest of the department thinks that Salem may have an accomplice. Someone from the inside, so don't trust anybody, you hear me, Q?"

Silence filled the airwaves as Grainger waited for an answer, hoping he'd take heed.

"I don't believe that, and by the tone of your voice, neither do you. I found a note on my car this morning."

"A note? From him? Why in the fuck didn't you report it?" Grainger was pissed now. Quinten had given up on life and, in turn, withheld valuable evidence.

"It said, *'Be patient,'* and he signed it as *'Venom.'* *Venom.* Only he would remember the jokes we taunted him with that day. Only a damaged child could hold onto something for that long, like me. I remember it vividly."

"Quinten, just listen to me. Don't you fucking give up. I can still stop this. Trust me!"

"Be safe, Dontarious. Now might be a good time to go get right with the Lord. You too can have peace and no longer fear Salem," Quinten said as he ended the call.

Grainger looked at the phone and shook his head. Quinten was always a tenacious fuck. This time, it would possibly cost him his life. Grainger didn't have time to worry about that anyway. He had to prove that Salem was still alive. He could've been anywhere, but Grainger knew for sure where he wasn't.

***

Pineview Cemetery was an eerie place to loiter around after dark, but that's any cemetery, for that matter. It was surrounded by trees on the outskirts of Rock City, earning its name, and served as the final rest stop for many fallen natives of the community. Grainger walked through the darkness, armed with a flashlight and his service weapon that dangled loosely in his holster. He was on a mission and wore it on his face like war paint. He had checked the database and found out a central location on the lot where the grave was, but it still would be a shot in the dark finding it.

He had no idea what he was going to do when he found what he was looking for; he was simply going off of a gut feeling that tossed and turn in the pit of his stomach. He needed to see it—or not see it. He needed proof that Salem was actually alive, and was determined to do anything to get it.

His light shined on each tombstone, looking for a familiar name or a clue that Salem faked his death. Part of him hoped that he wouldn't find the site; only because that part of him knew what the other part of him would do if he did. From side to side he shined his light like a conductor searching cargo cars for stowaways.

Near the far side of the lot, Grainger froze when he read the name on the tombstone.

SALEM KNIGHT
1986–2008
"HERE LIES THE TRUTH"

Grainger squinted as he read the tombstone and scanned the light around the grave. Something wasn't right, nothing sounded right, and only amplified suspicion was left. Grainger's detective senses kicked in. The tombstone looked far too new to be six years old, but there was always the chance that it had been recently replaced. The soil was a different issue. There wasn't a stone canvas, only a mound of dirt. A mound of *fresh* dirt, with footprints leading away from the scene. Grainger was on to something—he just needed to dig a little deeper.

He shined his light around the graveyard while gripping his pistol. He was expecting to see Salem standing off in the distance, smiling, and ecstatic that Grainger had played right into his plan—but all Grainger saw off in the darkness was an old shed that the caretaker probably used to store tools.

Let's find out how much truth is lying under here.

Grainger walked tactically across the lot and surprisingly found the shed to be unlocked. It was beginning to seem too easy. Maybe he *was* walking into a trap. He opened the door, shined his light while caressing the trigger on his weapon, and then disappeared into the shed. The old door slowly started closing behind him, and right before it was fully shut, it swung back open. Grainger peeked outside making sure the coast was clear, and exited dragging a shovel.

He propped his flashlight on the headstone and started unearthing the truth. He didn't have time to do the paperwork and strain his vocal cords trying to convince a judge to authorize a grave exhumation. He had to find out on his own, as always, and go from there. Every time he stabbed the earth, he visualized that he was holding a sword and injecting the blade into Salem's torso. As he piled a mound of dirt behind him, sweat poured down his face caking mud on his cheeks. His clothes naturally became filthy, and he started resembling a zombie . . . a zombie eagerly digging his own grave.

Hours passed by, and the moon retired as the sun began to rise. The sky turned orange. The crickets ceased chirping in the woods, replaced by morning birds taking over the mic. The chickens were finally coming home to roost. Grainger kept digging, taking minute rests at the edge of the six-foot deep hole that he dedicated his night to.

Finally, he gave Salem a final stab and struck a hard object. It was time. With a newfound flow of energy, Grainger uncovered the bland wooden casket. He stood to the side of it and tossed the shovel back to the surface as he pulled his pistol from his back. He had to laugh at himself; if Salem was in there, there was no way that he was alive.

Grainger squatted and grabbed the side opening of the casket and began to lift. It was heavier than he expected, or maybe he was far more exhausted than he realized. As he opened the casket he went to the edge and hopped up to grab his flashlight. The moment of truth was near, and he could feel his heart thumping like it was driving down a dirt road. Grainger shined the light in the casket and what he saw made him fall backward onto his ass. He quickly hopped up for a second look, praying that his mind was playing tricks on him . . . but this time it wasn't.

Officer Cherry's body was lying inside the fresh casket with a bullet in the center of his head. His arms were crossed and beneath his palms was a note.

Grainger poked him with the flashlight to make sure, and then grabbed the note from the late messenger.

"To Old Friends . . ."

Grainger ripped the note into confetti and screamed out of frustration at the top of his lungs. Salem was playing games, and he was, sadly, good at it, as he'd always been.

Pissed off for having his night wasted, Grainger climbed out of the grave, looked down, and spit on the open grave. His chest wheezed, and his arms hung low as he held his pistol and gritted his teeth at his display of failure. As he wiped his smutted forehead with the back of the hand that he held the pistol in, he heard a series of voices scream out at him.

"Drop the weapon and get down on the ground!" echoed through the stale air as numerous lights rushed toward him. Before he could speak, task force had him pinned face-first on the ground while placing him in cuffs.

"Chill! I'm a fucking cop, you idiots!" Grainger pleaded with what energy he had left.

A cop grabbed the weapon from his reach while two others stood him up. As Grainger tried to blink the soil from his eyes, he saw a slim figure walking toward him holding a blinding light in his face.

"Detective Grainger," the sweet voice said.

Grainger looked up as the figure came closer and into the light.

"Did you miss me?" Internal Affairs Agent Hackett asked with a malicious grin.

Cherry rushed across the graveyard with his uniform a complete mess. His shirt hung loosely over his belt and was tucked at the edges. His black gloves made his palms clammy and matched his drenched forehead that was wrinkled in worry. The walls were closing in on him, and suddenly he was having regrets about ever becoming an accessory to an old battle buddy's corrupt scheme.

He was meeting Salem in the back of the lot, their normal planning location, but this time was different. Cherry was no longer excited and eager to be an accomplice in Salem's psychotic crusade. They were friends and had been through a lot together in war and during the transition back to normal life, if you could call it that, but lately, Salem was getting out of hand. Cherry was in too deep to just walk away, especially now, but something had to be done to clear his name and preserve his innocence, or what was left of it.

He saw Salem sitting on his own tombstone, staring off into the distance as if the scenery was somewhat poetic to him. He didn't even break his glare when Cherry approached him in an exhausted jog.

"Aye, man, they hit me," Cherry said as he leaned over and caught his breath.

He expected a different response, or *some* response, but when he looked up, Salem was still looking off at the trees with a serene facial expression.

"You hear me? They hit my house! I think they got me on camera sneaking you into the hospital!"

"Did you get what I asked?" Salem still didn't make eye contact. He just sat there on the tombstone peacefully.

"What?" Cherry shook his head and dug into his pocket; it was the wrong pocket, so he reached into the other one.

He pulled out a pistol, Grainger's pistol, and handed it to Salem. "The dumb fuck left it in his car, unlocked. I made the switch and was back at my post before he even noticed."

Cherry was a different kind of guy than Salem, and Salem exploited that trait. Cherry was a follower. He was the type to find someone that he admired and follow them through what-

ever extremes that it took to gain their respect
and trust. Secretly, he was just looking to be
accepted, and Salem played on this card. Ever
since Afghanistan, Salem had manipulated
Cherry into assisting him in all of his dirty work,
including the faking of his death and sneaking
him out of that miserable country. It was there
that Salem found his true calling for violence.
The things that he witnessed and took part in
just opened up old wounds and old scars.

"Good work," Salem said as he examined the
weapon.

"So, what now? They're looking for me, and
I honestly don't know what to do now. It wasn't
supposed to be like this, Salem." Cherry stepped
closer and blocked his path of sight to whatever
he was looking at. "I was never supposed to get
found! The plan was to get rid of Grainger, and I
rise to his spot. That's what you promised me!"
Cherry said as he leaned forward and grabbed
Salem's shoulders. He tried to shake some sense
into him.

"Lower your voice and have some respect for
the dead," Salem responded. Cherry turned his
face up and looked around.

"Yo, I don't think you're taking this seriously,
guy. Open your eyes for once, Salem. This shit
is crumbling beneath our feet. It's over. What

started out as a dream has morphed into a fucking nightmare!" Cherry said as he turned around in frustration.

He glanced over the graveyard and shook his head. He was disappointed in himself for even getting caught up in such bullshit. Now his career was over, and so was his freedom—a fucking nightmare.

"You're forgetting something, though," Salem said as he stood up and covered his mouth in a yawn.

Cherry faced him and wondered what it could be. What was he forgetting, because Salem had to have a bigger plan, a next step, or something up his sleeve to clear their names. He was too calm, and Cherry was on the verge of an anxiety attack. "A nightmare is still a dream . . ."

Salem pointed the pistol at Cherry's head as the night drew silent. Cherry lowered his head, smiled, and looked back up.

"See, I knew you'd do that," Cherry said as he dug into his pocket. "I figured you'd try to kill me, so I switched the clip in the gun with an empty one," he said with a look of disappointment. He pulled the clip out of his pocket and held it up. What should've been a full clip that he swapped was now an empty one. Salem smiled at him while still holding the gun at his head. Cherry

raised his arms in surrender. He was defeated
and outsmarted. Salem must've switched the
clips back when Cherry was trying to shake some
sense into him. Cherry looked betrayed as his
face sank.

"The second mouse gets the cheese," Salem
said as he squeezed the trigger.

Grainger was being held in an interrogation
room, like a criminal. Salem had successfully
fucked his life over and turned the tables of
power as he DJ'd his playlist of revenge. This
whole time Grainger thought that he was getting
closer to catching Salem in a game of Freeze Tag,
but it turned out that Salem was playing musical
chairs.

Just a few weeks ago, Grainger was the man
around the precinct. Now he was shackled to
a metal table in filthy clothes and stripped of
his honor. He knew their interrogating tactics,
and he had been sitting in the bright room for
a few hours with not so much as a word from
anybody. He knew why he was there. He knew
what it looked like from the outside peeking
in, but they had to understand that the death
of Cherry wasn't his doing—directly. He was
already drained and on the brink of passing out,

but his adrenaline wouldn't allow him to close his eyes.

Finally the door opened and his worst nightmare walked in wearing a gray skirt and a purple blouse. Hackett's hair was now cut short and rested on her collar as her purple lipstick shined like a beacon on her pale skin. Her hair had changed, but her demeanor was still the same: power hungry, with an appetite for destruction, and taking a bite out of Grainger's career would be the perfect appetizer. She smiled at Grainger as she sat across from him and opened up a file. She crossed her smooth legs and placed her hand over her cleavage, as she seemed shocked at what she was reading.

"My, my, my, Detective. It seems as if some things never change," she said as she gazed over the rim of her glasses.

"It seems," Grainger responded as he looked away. He had spent too much time on the opposite side of the table with Hackett and knew her angle. She'd start off nice and flirtatious, and then quickly flip the script into her normal persona as a lumberjack to male ego.

"Tell me something." Hackett removed her glasses and folded them on top of the folder in front of her. She clasped her hands over her knee and began to rock in the chair as she stared at Grainger. "Why did you kill him?"

"Excuse me?" Grainger raised a brow as he tried to adjust himself in the restraints.

"Officer Cherry. Why did you kill him and try to cover it up in the last place you thought anyone would look? I have to admit, it was quite a clever tactic." She leaned forward on the table and spoke in a low, seductive tone to throw him off—that was her signature move. "Get your superiors started on a wild goose chase for someone who was already dead, and then stash the body of your accomplice in the empty grave. It has a certain romance to it, wouldn't you say?"

Grainger had to chuckle as his fatigued lungs pulsed air. "So that's the case you're trying to build? Cherry was my partner in crime, and *I* killed him?" He broke out into a fit of laughter only to mask the fury that was boiling in his tender veins. "You're asking the wrong questions here. You shouldn't ask why Cherry's body was in that grave, but better yet, ask why Salem's was not."

"That is none of my concern. You can lead your lieutenant on with that fairy tale, but not me. I know you, Grainger. You have always been a slick little fuck and a very manipulative but crafty criminal with a badge."

"Oh yeah?" Grainger smiled at her and shook his head.

"Absolutely." Hackett leaned back in the chair and folded her arms over her head. Her breasts nearly broke through the feeble buttons that were restraining them as she pretended to yawn. "Listen, we checked your gun . . ."

"And?"

"And it wasn't your gun. It was Cherry's serial number," Hackett said as she observed the confusion that spread over Grainger's face. "Since you're a man of theories, here's mine. You met up with Cherry when the heat fell on him. There was a scuffle. You ended up killing him with your gun—familiar, right?" Hackett hinted toward an earlier file.

Grainger shook his head and smiled at the camera in the top corner of the room that he knew was there. "Are y'all serious right now?"

"Then, to cover it up, you tried to bury his body, switched guns just in case, and was probably on your way back here to pencil whip the serial numbers in the log. Does that sound about right?" Hackett tapped her pen against the folder rapidly as she waited for a confession.

"Sounds like you are on dick withdrawal and taking it out on any man you see. What is your beef with me, Hackett? Is it because I would never fuck you? Is that it?" Grainger tried to spin the power role on her, but it didn't work.

"I don't fuck criminals," she said with a straight face. "But I will see you in court when I bend you over on that stand while the jury holds the camera. That's when you'll know that you've been fucked. Got it?"

The door burst open and in walked Cagle. He had a look of indignation on his face. He disliked Grainger, but hated Hackett. The last thing he wanted was Internal Affairs sticking their nose into his department's business. That's how his predecessor got canned.

"Hackett, do you have anything to actually hold this decorated detective with? Other than the fact he's an idiot who exhumed a grave without proper procedure?" Cagle asked as he walked behind Grainger and released him from the restraints. Grainger brought his wrists in front of him and start massaging them as he mugged Hackett.

"Not yet, but I will. As soon as that lab proves that the bullet that's in Cherry's head came from his gun," Hackett smiled at Grainger.

Grainger knew that it would come back to him. He had underestimated Salem, and chances are, he made the switch at the funeral somehow when Grainger left his weapon in the car. That bullet would come back to Grainger, no doubt, but he just needed a little more time to catch Salem first. He knew where he was going, but Grainger needed to protect his family first. He needed to get Julissa out of the city before Salem took his crusade to an all-time low.

"Well, until then, I'm placing him on admin leave," Cagle said as he helped Grainger to his feet. He grabbed him by the shoulders and looked him in the eyes.

"Detective, I strongly suggest that you go home and lay low. No more chasing this white whale. Let us take it from here and try to piece this shit that you unearthed back together. Do you understand?"

Grainger nodded and was just happy that Cagle finally had his back. He expected him to throw him to the wolves, one wolf in particular. Grainger smiled at Hackett as he was leaving the room.

"Another one for the files, Hackett," Grainger taunted as he closed the door and left the two inside to decide his fate.

Salem Says

Grainger parked his car a block from his house in the parking lot of a convenience store. He didn't want to take any chances of Salem finding him, or believing that he was home, so the precaution made sense at the time. The night was calm, with a gentle breeze that felt heavenly against his perspiring skin. The only things he wanted to do were get home, get Julissa out of town, shower, and figure out his next move. He had no faith in the judicial system, as ironic as it may have seemed, because he knew Salem was too smart to get caught now. The only way to close this case was to kill him; and after everything that Salem had put him through, Grainger was confident that when the time came, he'd be able to pull that trigger.

He was defenseless and wandering the streets in the attire of a failed thief—a failed grave robber. How did Salem know he would dig up that body? Grainger shook his head and sighed at the fact that the whole time Salem had been three steps and a skip ahead of him. Now he was walking down a dark street under trembling lamps, trying his best to throw his pursuer off his scent of fear.

Julissa wasn't answering her phone, but that was either normal for her being in a deep sleep or it was a sign that something was wrong. Salem wasn't fully predictable, but Grainger had a feeling that he wouldn't come for him until Quinten's tab of fate was fatally cleared. Still, he couldn't bank on that, so Grainger approached his house cautiously and looked for signs of foul play.

He opened the door quietly and stepped inside. Everything looked normal so far. The living-room light was on, as well as the light in the hallway, as the TV provided a backdrop for the eerie environment. Grainger retrieved a steak knife from the kitchen and headed toward the bedroom. His personal weapon was in the drawer of the nightstand, but he just had to make it there. He closed his eyes as he grabbed the knob and said a silent prayer that Julissa was okay. There was no telling what he would do if something happened to her. Other than the job, she was his reason to live, his only other passion than his profession.

He opened the door while gripping the knife with a sweaty palm and saw Julissa lying face-first on the bed—asleep, fully dressed, with an open book sliding from her fingertips. He walked over toward the bed while scanning the room and placed the knife down by his feet. Then he began to shake her as she slowly snapped back to coherence and rolled over. She opened one eye and smiled at him before snapping the other open and entering a state of fright.

"Dontarious, what happened to you?" she asked as she sat up and observed his appearance. He looked like he had been through shit, and he had. "You look like you've been playing in dirt!"

Grainger tried to smile and downplay the seriousness of the matter as he brushed off his rolled-up sleeves like it was nothing. "I'm okay, but listen. I need you to do something for me, for us," he said as he scooted closer. Julissa looked at him confused as she wiped a patch of mud from his cheek with her thumb. "Do you have somewhere that you can go? Like out of town? Just for a few days till I can figure some shit out."

Julissa raised a brow and frowned at him in a "What The Fuck?" look. "Figure some shit out? The hell are you talking about, 'do I have somewhere I can go?' What is this about, Dontarious?"

He could tell that her mind was in another lane, a highway to heartbreak hotel that he never planned on traveling with her. This was different, though. This was the bumpy asphalt of life or death with no exits in sight; a fuel tank empty of options, surrounded by fate's fog on four flat tires of hope.

"It's not like that, Lisa," Grainger said as he stood up and began pacing. He had no idea how he was going to explain it to her, but she needed to know the truth.

"Not like what? What is it like?" Her voice was low and serious now.

"Okay, there's a serial killer on the loose, and we have reason to believe that he may come for me and anyone close to me," he said as he leaned against the dresser. Julissa's mouth dropped as she stood in front of him.

"Does this . . . Does this have anything to do with your friends getting killed?"

"It has everything to do with that. That's why I need you to leave town until this blows over."

"Are you coming with me? Do they have a protective detail for you, or whatever it's called?" Julissa's eyes widened as she was on the brink of anxiety. "Okay, okay, okay, let me think. I know where we can go." She raked her fingers through her loose locks and tilted her head back in thought. "Let's go to—"

"I can't go with you, Lisa," he cut her off. She turned and shot him a concerned look as her hand naturally levitated to her hip.

"What do you mean you're not coming with me?"

"I have to stay here and finish this. Plus, I'm on admin hold until this is over. I kind of got into some shit," he lowered his head.

"Kinda? Uhhh . . . I'd say so. You have some lunatic trying to kill you, and now you want me to leave you here by yourself? Fuck that." It was very rare that Julissa cursed, so Grainger knew she was heated. "Some psycho is after your family," she mumbled as she began pacing. She stopped and pointed at him. "You either come with me, or I'm staying here with you. We'll get through this shit together, as a family."

"I can't let you do that, Lisa. I can't focus on catching this guy if I have to worry about your safety."

"Catch him? The hell are you smoking, Dontarious? We need to get as far away from this shit as we can. We can go to Maryland. We can stay with my girl Lamia till this is over. Till the police do their job and find that asshole."

"I *am* the police. It is *my* job to catch him," Grainger said as he stepped from the dresser and walked toward the nightstand. He opened the drawer and took out his pistol and checked the magazine for ammunition.

"Not right now you're not. You're on admin hold, remember? They took you off the case for a reason, Dontarious, and it damn sure wasn't for you to go chase this guy. Stop being so stubborn and come with me." Julissa opened the closet and began packing a few essential items for the trip. She stopped and looked over her shoulder and saw Grainger still sitting on the bed, looking over the pistol. "Get ready. We're leaving . . ." she spoke in her tone of authority.

Usually it would work on Grainger . . . if she was referring to cutting the grass or tagging along with her shopping, but his mind was too far gone. He didn't trust the department to find Salem. It had to be him.

"Julissa, listen to me! Pack whatever you need for a few days and get out of town. I have to stay here. I have to finish this. I just . . . I just have to . . ."

Julissa stood up with a small luggage case in her grasp. She stared at Grainger and read the expression on his face. He was dead set, and there was nothing she could say to make him change his mind. It's just how he was.

"You don't 'have' to do shit but stay alive for your family, for me, and anyone else that cares about you." Julissa walked toward the door and turned back toward him. "But you don't see that. You're blinded by blood, and the only thing you care about is the job. You're not taking this seriously. You never do." Grainger looked up at her and saw the pain in her brown eyes. "You only care about closing another major case and putting another staple in your precious file."

"You know that's not true. I love you. That's why I can't risk anything happening to you if you stay," Grainger said as he stepped to her and placed his hands on her shoulders. "Why can't you understand that?"

"Love is a two-way street, Dontarious. What about how *I* feel? What about the risk that *I'm* taking if you stay? Why can't you understand *that?*" He let go and took a step back as he squeezed his temples in indecisiveness.

"Your mind is made up already, and there's nothing I can say to change it. So fuck it. You stay here and do whatever you have to do. I won't stick around and be a 'liability,' as you put it. Just know that if something happens to you, I will be more hurt than you would if the tag was on the other toe."

She exited the room as Grainger followed her to her car in silence. As she hopped in and started it, he stood at the driver-side window with his head on a swivel for suspicious activity.

She started backing up, but he held onto the window as she almost dragged him before stopping with a deep sigh.

"What? I'm leaving—just like you wanted!" she snapped.

"Stop talking like that, Lisa. You know it's not like that at all."

"Then what is it like?" Julissa shook her head into her palms as she felt tears begin to swell up in irritated sockets. She wiped them away and looked at Grainger with red eyes.

"Don't answer that . . . 'cause I know you can't. Bye, Dontarious." She started backing up slowly all while maintaining eye contact. "If this is the end, remember that I love you," she said as she stopped at the mailbox. Grainger looked at her, and then at the mailbox—the flag was up.

"I love you too, and trust me . . . This isn't the end . . . Everything will be back to normal soon, okay?" Grainger said as he walked over staring at the mailbox.

"That's what I'm afraid of . . ." Julissa shook her head and drove off.

He watched her taillights disappear into the night, and then snapped his attention toward the mailbox as he snatched it open. Inside he found a note . . .

*Simon Says, be patient . . . Your turn is near.
Don't worry about your girlfriend. She isn't
on my list. Not this one.*

Toni sat at the edge of Quinten's bed as she
stared at herself in the full mirror on the wall.
Her mind was drag racing her heartbeat, and she
couldn't see a finish line in sight. She had no idea
what she was doing with her life, where she was
going with her life, because she had wasted so
much time living "her life." As a young lady with
a thirst for adrenaline, she had found herself
lost down a dark path with no one to turn to for
guidance. It seemed as if death was following
her: from Scott, to Neka, to the random guy
in VIP. Maybe she was cursed. Maybe she was
destined to be alone and God was removing any
and everyone that she became close to. *If that is
true, then what's to become of Quinten?*

Quinten slid behind her until she was between
his legs and wrapped his arms around her. He
sniffed her skin and held in the potent whiff
of her natural fragrance until he was naturally
high. He could tell something was on her mind,
and he obviously knew what it was, just not
how deep her well of secrets really went. He too
had lost a friend, a few of them, in fact, but he
couldn't help but wonder if they deserved to die.
If that was so, then what was to become of him?

"You okay, T?" Quinten asked as he started massaging her tense shoulders.

Her skin was smooth and warm to the touch as he began kissing on the back of her neck. Toni closed her eyes and tried to ignore the signals that her body was receiving and transmitting. His full lips on the nape of her neck made her pussy drool, but she wasn't in the mood for sex. She was horny, but not in the mood for sex.

He barely got a spare moment alone with his girl these days, and lately, it had been taking a toll on him. He knew she was in Greensboro doing her thing, and he was cool with that. Some people viewed him as a fool for love, pussy whipped, or whatever other cliché that could be used to describe his fascination over Toni, but he didn't care. He didn't care about the other guys that she's used as hobbies, just something to do to pass time. As long as her heart remained with him, Quinten was satisfied.

It wasn't like he was an ugly guy. He worked out daily, was toned, had pecan skin and the eyes to match, and more than a handful of ladies made advances at him, but he was loyal to Toni. She had his heart, even if it was on reserve, nationally guarded, and only showed up on the weekends.

"I'm sorry, Q, but I have to leave . . ." Toni said as she stood up and started collecting her things from the dresser.

Quinten looked at her confused and wondered what the rush was to get back to Greensboro. He stood up and stepped behind her as he wrapped his arms around her again.

"Have you seen my phone?" she asked as she spun around and faced him. Her hair was mangled, and she looked like devastation in the flesh, but she was still beautiful to Quinten.

"I must have left it in the car."

"Look, calm down, T. What's the rush anyway?" he asked with a seductive smile as he pulled her closer to his chest. She leaned back as if she was resisting, but the sensation of his tongue flickering on her throat made her knees weak for a brief moment.

"I just need to get back. There's some things that I have to handle early in the morning," she lied as she backed her head away.

She could see it in his eyes that he knew she wasn't faithful, and that's what made the situation even more awkward. How could he love her so much, when she offered so little? She didn't deserve his affection. She didn't deserve his gifts of romance and cloud nine kisses, but a lot of people oftentimes received what they didn't deserve—like Neka. Toni was the one who deserved to be in that grave.

"Come on now, I barely get time to see you anymore," Quinten said as he placed a soft kiss on her lips. "You show up for one day, and then vanish like you were never here." He kissed her neck again. That was her spot and a remote to open her mouth in a passionate *ahh,* like a garage door. "Just let me please my woman real quick. Then you can leave, if you still want to," he suggested as he grabbed her waist and lifted her into the air.

She tried to fight back her smile, but her cheek muscles seemed to override her inner demons. He placed her down at the edge of the bed and kneeled before her like the queen he envisioned.

"Q, stop. I have to—" she tried to speak, but his tongue sliding beneath the waist of her sweats made her sweat, and made her core temperature rise like mercury.

He undid her drawstrings and slid her pants to her ankles, freeing one foot as he stood up and rubbed his hand along her freshly shaven skin. He took her pink-painted toes and placed them in his mouth one by one as he sucked the little piggies home. To be a religious square on the outside, Quinten too had a lustful demon that he kept packed away.

"I know that you're going through something, but let me make it right," he said as he slithered his tongue up her thigh like a snake entering the Garden of Eden.

Her forbidden fruit began to melt. Like a homeless man receiving his first meal in weeks, he started devouring her liquids like a hearty soup, turning her legs into nimble strands of noodles. Her moans bounced off the walls and ricocheted into his eardrums as he flicked his tongue against her clit like a boxer warming up.

She tried to tighten her thighs to fight back her orgasm, but he pried them apart and turned his torture up a notch. He entered two fingers inside her as it caught her off guard and made her gasp and fall flat on her back. She grabbed his scalp and massaged his ears as his tongue ice-skated making figure eights as he consumed her melting lake. She closed her eyes, and they instantly popped back open when his tongue made contact with her asshole. His warm gland felt heavenly against her rectum as he spread her cheeks and fucked her with his tongue while still fingering her.

The stars aligned perfectly, and for a short second in the universe, she forgot about her problems as he explored her Milky Way with his index finger and continued teasing her moon. A chill shot through her body like a shooting star as she shivered into a powerful nut that sent her brain into a black hole. She was so caught up in the ecstasy that she forgot to make a wish. She came all over his fingers, and then came all over again. Even with all of the guys that she practiced infidelity with, none of them made her feel like Quinten did—she felt loved, and she hated herself for that.

He stood up and smiled at her with glossy lips as her reality rushed back to her face. Immediately, she put her sweats back on and grabbed her things with an embarrassed look as she scrambled like the apartment was on fire . . . really, it was her conscience.

"What's wrong? You didn't like it?" Quinten asked confused. She was treating him like a one-night stand . . . like a dude who gets head and just leaves . . .

"No, Quinten, I loved it, and that's the problem," Toni said as she exited the room.

He followed her to the door with his mouth stuck on stupid. He couldn't even begin to muster anything to say to her. She opened the door and turned to him as if she was going to say something, but didn't as she closed it. Quinten stared at the door for what felt like forever as he tried to decipher what had just happened, or what he had done wrong. His dull mind drew a blank as he shook his head and locked the door behind her. If that was how she wanted it, then that's how he was going to treat her from then on—like a casual fuck.

He headed toward the shower but stopped in the bedroom to grab a towel. As he was walking out, he noticed his phone light up on the dresser so he checked it. It was Toni.

"Hey, baby, I left my keys up there. Unlock the door."

He tossed the phone on the dresser and headed toward the front. Toni was beginning to show signs of being bipolar, but he wasn't in the mood to deal with her anymore that night. He unlocked the door and headed back to hop in the shower. As he took off his shirt and pulled his pants down in the bathroom, he smiled at his semihard dick and the lustful hopes that he had of her joining him in the shower. She had a hold on him, and he had to admit it. It was like his heart was locked, and only she had the—He froze as a daunting thought flickered in his brain. *If she left her keys up here, then how did she get her cell phone?*

Quinten pulled his pants back up and rushed out to the living room. The tall figure in all-black that was standing before him froze him in his tracks like he had turned to a pillar of salt. The sound of his tongue clicking against the roof of his mouth in a "tsk, tsk!" sound sent chills through the room. Quinten had let his guard down in wartime, and now he was staring face-to-face with Salem.

Quinten slowly started stepping backward as he planned on making a dash for his phone on the dresser. Salem was standing with his thumbs tucked into the front of his belt as his cold eyes watched Quinten's pathetic attempt at an escape.

Then Salem pulled a pistol from his waist, and Quinten nearly fell over the couch when he saw death staring him in the face. He raised his hands in surrender as sweat leaked down his chin and trickled down his bare chest.

"Speak the devil's name, and death shall occupy your living room." Salem offered an ominous smirk as he bit the inside of his bottom lip. "Don't look so shocked to see me. We both knew this was inevitable."

"Salem, what do you want?" Quinten asked as he eyeballed the pistol in his hand.

The once-lanky kid who everyone made fun of was now molded into a killer. Who could hold on to a grudge for that long? If this was God's plan, then Quinten had to accept it. There was nothing he could do about it at that point.

"That's rhetorical," Salem answered.

Suddenly, Toni rushed inside the apartment with her face focused on the contents of her purse.

"Where in the hell is my phone!" she shouted furiously at herself.

She didn't even notice Salem till she looked up, and it was too late. Salem grabbed her by her hair as she cried out, and tilted her head back into the light. He observed her familiar face and smiled at her.

"Interesting," he said before he shoved her toward Quinten.

She struggled for her footing in the momentum, as Quinten caught her in a strong embrace. Salem tossed a bundle of rope at Quinten's feet and nodded toward a small desk chair off in the corner.

"Tie her up, and don't try any funny shit."

"What's going on, Quinten?" Toni asked with panic in her tone.

He looked at Salem, the gun, and then at Toni's face. Her innocent face—she didn't deserve what was happening to her.

"Let her go, Salem. This is between us, right?" Quinten said as he helped Toni with her balance.

"Man, stop with all that lovey-dovey bullshit. I have another stop to make tonight, and your stalling is counterproductive," Salem said. He cocked the gun back and pointed it in their direction, making Toni bury her face in Quinten's chest. "Hurry up, Quinten."

Knowing that he was out of options, Quinten did as he was instructed. His only hope was that Salem would simply take his life, but spare his heart. Salem walked over and observed the knot that restrained Toni, and then shoved Quinten toward the couch. The sound of Toni's cries broke Quinten's heart as he sat on the couch and watched her eyes fog with tears.

"She doesn't deserve this," he said as he looked up at Salem who was standing behind her.

"But you do," Salem said as he tucked the pistol back into his waist and pulled out a six-inch blade. He held it up to the light like he was inspecting utensils out of a dishwasher. "You deserve to watch someone you love beg for their life, while standing back silently and watching like the noble citizen you are." Salem pulled a roll of duct tape from his cargo pocket and tore a strip off with his teeth. Toni tried to shake her head to resist until she saw the blade in her face as he applied the tape on her mouth.

Salem squatted behind Toni and grabbed the top of her head as he placed the backside of the knife on her throat. Her screams were muffled as she felt the cold steel make contact with her soul.

"So this is how things are going to work." Toni's posture stiffened as he applied pressure. "All you have to do is tell her that you don't love her," Salem said.

Quinten sat on the edge of the couch ignoring the pain he was in. His physical state wasn't important at the moment. The life of the woman he loved was being threatened, and there wasn't a thing he could do about it. "Toni, baby, don't worry. I'm going to get us out of this," he pleaded fretfully, but even he didn't believe his words.

"Not likely . . ." Salem remarked.

"Baby, I promise I—"

"Stop fucking around!" Salem snapped. "All you have to say is, 'I don't love you,' and I will spare her worthless life. I only aim to kill loved ones."

Quinten looked up at Salem, then back at Toni. Her eyes were gone, smothered by cloudy tears in a shit storm that he forecasted but still stayed in the path of Hurricane Salem. This debt was his to pay; not hers.

"I don't think I believe you," Quinten said.

He was just trying to buy time till he thought of another escape route. There wasn't one, though. His life had hit a roadblock for him and his passenger, and they were now staring at death's detour.

"I don't think you have a choice," Salem responded in a stoic tone.

"Baby, I swear I'm—" Quinten started as he reached out for her.

Salem flipped the knife over to the sharp edge and applied slight pressure. Trickles of blood cascaded down, as well as stifled shrieks.

"Okay, okay, okay!" Quinten yelled as he restrained himself and rubbed the sweat from his eyes.

"Toni," he started and looked up into Salem's eyes. "I . . . I don't love you . . . I don't love you, Toni. I never did . . ." Quinten said.

The words stung as they escaped his lips. He loved her with all of his heart, and even though she knew the truth behind his statement, it hurt to say such a thing.

"See? That wasn't so difficult," Salem said as he released her chin.

Her head rocked forward, but her body was motionless, except for the tears that continued to pour and her nostrils that flared for oxygen. The sight of her in so much anguish made Quinten drop his head. "Shame though, the last thing she heard in this world was you saying that you don't love her."

Quinten lifted his head up in shock. He saw the muscles in Salem's arm tense up as he grabbed Toni's head and put the blade to her throat. It was too late for Quinten to do anything about fate, so he just closed his eyes and gritted his teeth. He was waiting to hear something—anything—whatever death sounded like, but the room was silent. Slowly he opened his eyes and saw Salem and Toni staring at him in the same position.

"You need to see this," Salem said as he snatched the blade across her throat, flinging red chaos upon the walls.

Jet streams of blood shot out from her jugular as her screams ceased. Quinten's heart stopped as he jumped to his feet and looked at the love of his life as she bled out and slumped her head over. Salem stood up and kicked her body over to the side as he mugged Quinten while holding the bloody knife to his side.

Without even knowing what he was doing, Quinten stepped forward and reached pathetically for Toni's body as she lay on the floor in a pool of her own plasma. As he got closer, Salem grabbed him by the throat and squeezed so hard that tears sprouted out of Quinten's eyes. Then he shoved him backward. Quinten fell over the glass coffee table, shattering it on impact. He could hear glass breaking beneath Salem's boots as he stepped closer. With what little strength he had left, Quinten rolled over on his back as fragments of glass stuck to his skin like preschool glitter. He looked up at his killer and closed his eyes as he began to make peace with God.

"Our Father in heaven, hallowed be your name, your kingdom come, your will be done, on earth as it is in heaven. Give us this day our daily bread. Forgive us our debts, as we also have forgiven our debtors. And lead us not into temptation, but deliver us from the evil one. For if you forgive men when they sin against you, your Heavenly Father will also forgive you. But if you do not forgive men their sins, your Father will not forgive your sins," Quinten mumbled the scripture.

"So you choose to resort to biblical reasoning?" Salem asked as if he was intrigued by the plea.

He leaned over, grabbed Quinten by his shoulders, and propped him against the couch—forcing him to look at him. For the first time, up close, Quinten could see the pain that was in Salem's eyes. He knew the goofy little kid was in there somewhere, hiding behind the monster he had become. The one that he was forced to become.

"Put your sword back in its place . . . for all who draw the sword will die by the sword. Do you think that I cannot call on my Father, and he will at once put at my disposal more than twelve legions of angels? Matthew 26:52–53, NIV." Salem recited his own choice of scripture. "Well, Quinten, appeal to your Lord and let's see these so-called legions of angels. Don't worry, I'll wait."

Salem retreated to a recliner in the corner and crossed his legs. Moments of silence filled the apartment as he sat with his head on a swivel as if he was actually expecting something to happen.

"Man, Quinten, I tell ya, I don't think they're coming," Salem said as he got up and approached him again. He grabbed Quinten's face until they were eye level. "Your God has abandoned you to die. How does that feel?"

Cops & Robbers

Grainger was stretched across his couch as the TV played at a low volume. He hadn't glanced at it in hours. He was lying on his back, tossing a basketball in the air repeatedly, as his mind was anywhere but in that house. He felt as if he should be out doing something—anything—but what? There was nothing that he could do. He had no chance in finding Salem unless he showed up at his front door, and that was the plan that Grainger was banking on. He looked over and made sure that his pistol was still on the coffee table.

There was a flaw to his plan, though. He knew before Salem would go after him, he would kill Quinten first. Grainger hated the fact that Quinten didn't take his warning and leave town, which was ironic, because a part of him wanted to escape with Julissa. Deep inside, he knew that wasn't the way things were meant to play out. He had to end this. He was anxious to seal this case and rub it in Hackett's face, again, but the waiting process was beginning to take a toll on him.

Grainger rested the ball on his chest as he glanced at his watch. It was a cheap Timex, with a brown Velcro band that most men of his age would commit suicide before wearing. That watch was different, though. It was given to him by his father, and ever since his death, he had worn it 24/7, even in the shower.

He wondered how things came to this. Just a few weeks ago, he was being awarded for his civil service, and now, he had fallen back into his normal routine as a fuckup. He was back on admin hold, with another case weighing heavily on his heart. The last case was different. He could've walked away from that one at any time, but not this one, not when he was a target and a grand finale to a killer's prestige. Grainger shook his head and began tossing the ball back into the air. He hoped that Julissa was okay and that one day she would understand his reasoning and his passion for a job that obviously didn't give a fuck about him.

His phone vibrated against the wood of the coffee table, so he reached over and checked it. The name on the screen made him sit up as he opened the text.

Dontarious, where are you? We need to meet, Quinten sent.

Grainger started to reply and tell him to come over, but a thought barricaded his fingers and made him erase what he started to send. He couldn't help but think the worst. What if Salem had already killed Quinten and was now using his phone? The risk was surreal, but real enough that he couldn't play against those odds.

Call me is how he replied. He would be able to tell from his voice if he was under duress. Grainger held the phone and waited till it lit back up. It wasn't a call like he expected, but another message.

Can't. I think he's here. I need help, man. Can you come save a friend?

That was it. The message sounded suspect, and Grainger wasn't about to fall for it. It was official. Quinten was dead, and Salem was now on the hunt for Grainger. It wouldn't be long before he showed up at his house to collect Karma's debt. Grainger grabbed his pistol and dashed toward the window. He peeked out of the blinds cautiously, looking for anything out of the norm but found nothing.

Hold on, I'm sending backup to your house. What's your address? Grainger sent, just to see how Salem would respond.

Are you home? was the response that he received.

Grainger shook his head and peeked back out the window as he held his gun up like the legendary photo of Malcolm X. He wasn't about to go out like that. He wanted to lure Salem in for the kill, but his methods were beginning to confuse Grainger. Why play games? He obviously knew where Grainger lived, so why try to bait him out?

Nah, I left town with my girl. You should've done the same like I warned you. It hurt Grainger to send that message. What if he was wrong? What if Quinten was actually hiding in a closet, scared for his life and reaching out for a friend? The irony was too much to swallow, so he proceeded to call the incident in. As soon as he was starting to dial the direct number to the dispatch line, he received another message. His curiosity opened it.

You're right. I should've, but I didn't believe shit till it came to my door. Grainger frowned at the riddle—until the knock at his door startled him. He carefully walked over to it with his gun raised as he looked through the peephole. The image on the other side made him gasp. He saw

Quinten's face covered in blood. Without thinking, Grainger snatched the door open to help a friend—until he saw an old friend standing behind Quinten. Shock turned his muscles into cement as he stood there in disbelief.

"Dontarious!" Salem shouted as if he was excited to see him.

He was. He only dragged Quinten along and used the texting gimmick to add a sense of betrayal to the bullet he planned on gifting him.

"I'm sorry," Quinten mumbled with eyes of fatigue.

Grainger looked at him as a bullet ripped through Quinten's back and came out his chest. Grainger fell to the floor as the shot barely missed him and dropped his gun in the process. He looked up and saw Quinten's eyes gradually shut as he collapsed to his knees and fell over. All Grainger could see now was Salem's smoking gun.

"Dontarious," Salem said, as he seemed to look around the house. "Can you have company?"

Grainger took advantage of the moment and grabbed his pistol. He rolled over and fired three shots where Salem was originally standing in the doorway, but the figure was gone. In a panic, Grainger scrambled to his feet and ran to the back of the house. He ducked off into his bedroom and took cover in the threshold. The image of Quinten lying lifeless on the floor was stained in Grainger's eyelids. Every time he blinked he saw his old friend, and another memorial of failure.

"I don't know what you want, Salem, but this won't end the way you planned it, I promise you that," Grainger shouted.

He could hear Salem's boots as he entered the house and tucked off into the kitchen. He was no doubt planning to take cover in the living room, and they both had straight lines of sight down the hallway. Grainger had been in this position many times, but each scenario felt different. This one was personal, and his chances of escape were dwindling with each shot he wasted. He peeked out into the hallway and fired another two shots into the distance. The echo was deafening within the walls of the small house, but that was the least of Grainger's worries at the moment.

Grainger bounced back into cover and frowned his face up when he heard two shots fly his way. They both stood with their backs against the wall of the living room and the master bedroom.

Only a few square feet separated them. Well, a bathroom. Grainger knew he had to keep track of Salem or he could enter the bedroom through the bathroom door that led right behind him.

"Just like old times, huh, Dontarious?" Grainger listened and tried to guess Salem's position. "Cops and robbers, right?" Salem yelled through the dark hallway. His static voice resonated. "Like kids again, you remember that?" Salem waited for an answer.

Grainger leaned over and tried to feel for the house phone on the nightstand, but, of course, it wasn't there. Instead, he successfully knocked over his alarm clock. Salem answered to the movement with two more shots, sending Grainger sliding back in to cover his ass.

Grainger reached his arm out and squeezed three more times. His eardrums were adjusting to the racket of combustion now. The smell of gunpowder polluted the air as Grainger could feel his rib cage inflating with his heartbeat. He needed to calm down if he planned on landing a shot. He waited for the echoes to settle, and then listened for positioning. He had no idea how this would end, but he knew he had to come up with a plan fast.

"You always had to be the cop. Always had to be the good guy, the hero, and what does that leave me?" Salem asked as they traded more shots.

"Right! A villain! You made me this way. *You* are responsible!" Salem yelled.

Grainger fired two more shots. At this point, he was wondering if he was wasting ammo or successfully pinning his pursuer down. Whatever the case was, he wouldn't be able to do it much longer. He kept his ears toward the hallway for movement and kept a steady eye on the bathroom entrance to his bedroom.

The house became quiet. Only slight movement from the living room riddled the night. Grainger felt his wrist and pushed the button on his watch illuminating the face for a brief second. He noticed that the glass on the watch had cracked and only a small piece of it remained lodged intact. He shook his head; he really loved that watch. His childish thought made him frown as he snapped back into the seriousness of the matter at hand.

"Aye, Grainger, look! I'm serious, time-out! Check this shit out."

Grainger was mystified. Was Salem really that loony to call a "time-out" during an actual shoot-out? Was this really a game to him? How could Grainger plan on formatting a logical escape route when his adversary had never grasped the full understanding of logic itself?

Grainger untrustingly peeked out for a millisecond and returned to cover.

"No, no, I'm serious, man. Check this shit out. You gon' die laughing, no pun intended," Salem said in a childish manner.

Grainger glanced out and waited for his eyes to adjust to the darkness. Down the hall he saw that Salem was dangling something out in the open. It was an old photo of Grainger's mother that Salem must have taken off the wall.

"Y'all boys better get out of my damn garden playing with those sticks!" Salem said in a motherly voice while tilting the portrait side to side as if it was really talking as he burst out into an animated cackle. There he was, a cold-hearted killer, snickering over childhood reminiscences. "You remember that shit, man? Your fucking moms would come outside yelling at us and shit. Good times, man . . . Good times."

Grainger stood up, remaining behind cover, and thought to himself, *This guy has really lost it*. He checked his clip quietly and let out a deep sigh at what he saw.

"You see, the way I have observed this scenario is that your pistol, your subcompact 9 mm, only holds ten rounds. And that, my friend, puts you at empty," Salem proclaimed. The seriousness had returned to his tone. "So nothing is to stop me from running over there and cancelling your subscription on life!" he screamed.

"This isn't you, Salem. You're not a killer. You're just a lost kid that never grew up." Grainger was trying to keep Salem talking to buy time.

"You sure about that?" Salem asked. "I mean, maybe the latter. We all pretend to be something that we aren't, isn't that right?" Grainger was looking around the room trying to remember if he had any extra ammo, but his mind was drawing blanks—underscores underlined in blood. "So who are you, Dontarious? You pretend to be this supercop, but I know the real you. I've seen your other disguises."

Grainger could hear Salem moving. He glanced at his bedroom window, and that seemed like the only way out. Sure, he could dash over, but by the time he unlocked it and pried it open from the old layers of paint from years of being shut, Salem would have a gun at the back of his head.

He was merely a moth caught up in fate's web, and now along came a spider.

"So, Dontarious! Tell me, are you Alex Cross or are you Tyler Perry?" Salem shouted.

Grainger heard movement in the hall and started to smile. Salem was rushing him and didn't account for the fact that Grainger's pistol could hold eleven if he cocked one in the chamber. Now Salem's cockiness was about to earn him one in the head.

Grainger knew he had one shot left. He heard commotion coming toward him and knew Salem was charging for the finish. He knew he had to make the final shot count, so he timed the footsteps, stepped out, and fired his last shot—directly into his basketball that was bouncing his way. He had been bamboozled . . .

Once he realized what had happened, he snapped his head around—and Salem was standing right behind him. He had come in through the bathroom entrance and now sported a wicked yet childish grin on his face. "We all ignore the skeletons in our closet until they start moving," Salem said as he seized Grainger by the throat. All Grainger could see was the small chrome pistol in his face and the metallic gleam in Salem's sick eyes.

Salem clutched Grainger's throat until his fingernails began to dig into his flesh and pinned him against the wall. It wasn't the pain that immobilized Grainger . . . It was the sheer embarrassment of being outfoxed once again. Now he was staring death in the face as his reaper offered nothing emotionally but a sadistic grin while Grainger clawed at his grip to no avail.

"Do you even value your life?" Salem asked as he leaned closer. Grainger could feel his brain responding to the lack of oxygen as his vision began to blur. "Here's a tip, never value anything that can be taken away from you, and *anything* can be taken away from you."

Grainger built up all of the energy that his weakening muscles could offer and head butted Salem. The strike caught his captor off guard, and he loosened his grip just enough to allow a short gust of air into Grainger's body—but that was enough. Before Salem could respond, Grainger swung a wild haymaker, but Salem ducked it and slammed Grainger's head into the wall, creating an imprint in the drywall. Still restrained by his neck, Grainger was helpless as the déjà vu returned.

Salem tucked his pistol and retrieved a knife from his back as he held it up to the moonlight shining in through the window. Grainger couldn't help but stare at it as he saw his own pitiful reflection in the blade—but also something else near the bed as the edge rotated. Salem held it to his neck, right above his hand, and applied gradual pressure. Grainger grimaced at the pain as his vision began to haze once again.

"Have you ever heard of those friendship tattoos?" Salem asked as he slightly cut into Grainger's neck. "I have my own way of—"

His statement was interrupted by a kick to his nuts that sent Salem faltering backward as he hunched over, holding his prize jewels. The pain subsided as he began to chuckle at Grainger's desperate attempt. Grainger dashed over to the bed and practically somersaulted across the mattress. Salem thought he was going for a gun, but Grainger pulled out a wooden baseball bat that Julissa kept on her side of the bed—she hated guns—Grainger hated that she hated guns and preferred that she had a shotgun on her side of the bed, just for the rare type of situation that he was currently in.

"I told you this wouldn't end like you thought," Grainger said in a weak pitch as his body was slowly regaining its strength.

"Oh yeah?" Salem said as he stood back up straight and smiled. "I've already written this story before. Many times over in my head," Salem said as he took small careful steps toward him. Grainger gripped the bat over his shoulder as if he was waiting for a pitch and wondered why Salem wasn't going for his gun. "The first draft is always shit," Salem said as he leisurely inched closer. Grainger gauged the distance and waited till the stars aligned up just right, and then he made a wish.

"Writing the story is only half the battle," Grainger said. Salem's eyebrow rose as he became intrigued. "What's a writer without a good editor?" Grainger continued as he swung the bat right for Salem's head.

Salem ducked, sending Grainger spinning in momentum, and punched him in the side of his rib cage, but the bat returned and struck him in the shoulder. Grainger swung again, the opposite direction this time, and struck Salem's other shoulder, sending him stumbling to the side. Thinking that he was finally getting the upper hand, Grainger hopped over the mattress and swung for the finale, but his strike was caught by Salem's bare hand as he smiled at him—he was merely toying with his food.

"Welcome to Draft Two," Salem said as he offered his own head butt directly into Grainger's nose, forcing him to fall onto the bed, clouding his judgment as blood rained from his nostrils.

As he opened his eyes, Grainger saw Salem dashing over to him with the bat raised above his head like a livid lumberjack. As soon as he came down with the weapon aimed for Grainger's skull on the chopping block, Grainger lifted his feet and kangaroo kicked Salem in his chest. The force wasn't life-threatening, but it saved Grainger's life . . . for the moment.

Grainger rolled off the bed as Salem sprawled back and bumped into the dresser. He was still smiling, but didn't seem to notice that his pistol had fallen from his waist in the commotion—Grainger knew that was his only chance. He backed against the wall as Salem rushed forward and swung for his head. Timed perfectly, Grainger ducked as the bat lodged into the plaster. He tumbled under Salem's reach and grabbed the pistol as he slid across the carpet and aimed the gun. He slowly stood to his feet as he caressed the trigger. He should've just shot him there, but for some eccentric reason, Grainger was hoping Salem would give up and face his wrongs in court.

Salem turned around and began to chuckle as he walked toward Grainger, rotating the bat at his side.

"Salem! It's over! Please don't make me kill you!" Grainger shouted. Salem just continued smiling as he spread his arms out.

"Go ahead, shoot. Pull the fucking trigger!" Salem dared him.

Grainger tightened his grip and steadied his aim. "Salem, trust me, I'll do it. Please don't force me to take that route."

"Please? Please? Do you hear yourself?" Salem asked as he propped the bat behind his neck and rested his arms over it. "The man with the gun is saying 'please'? You're begging for my life? You don't see the irony in that?"

Grainger shook his head slowly as he bit down on his lip.

"Or maybe," Salem looked down at the floor, and then up at Grainger, "maybe the badge has made you weak. Maybe you're now realizing that it's much easier to watch someone pull the trigger, than it is to do it yourself."

"Salem, trust me, I'll kill you." Grainger warned.

"Like you killed your partner?" Salem asked.

The random reminder of history shocked Grainger and temporarily disabled his response. His "Jump Out Boys" days were a dark chapter in his life that he didn't want to revisit. Salem's smile widened when he looked at Grainger's reaction with drooped cheeks.

"See that?" Salem said as he pointed with the bat at Grainger's face. "That is remorse! That is guilt! That is sorrow! That is feeling bad for killing a friend."

"Cut the mind games, Salem, before I end this shit tragically. I promise I will!"

"Do it!" Salem grinned. "Here, I'll give you a reason for your precious file," he said as he gripped the bat in attack mode and walked toward Grainger.

"Salem!"

"Do it!"

As Salem cocked back and went to swing, Grainger aimed, closed his eyes, and pulled the trigger.

Click!

He opened his eyes and looked at the pistol in misery as Salem smiled at him. "You should really learn your weapons, Dontarious."

Salem swung the bat and connected with Grainger's knee, sending him buckling in agony. With no options left and pain ricocheting through his joints, Grainger lodged the empty pistol at Salem's head, but it missed and struck the mirror. Grainger watched as his reflection crumbled into confetti and celebrated his failure. Salem cocked back and swung the bat at Grainger's back in a deafening thump that made him face plant onto the carpet in defeat.

Grainger blinked slowly as his nose began to bleed again. He lay there as the warm blood puddled around his cheek. It felt soothing, or maybe that feeling was death creeping up his spine. His tranquil eyes bulged open in anguish as Salem dug his knee into his spine and rested on him. Salem wedged the bat under Grainger's throat and held both sides like a rein of torture. He began to pull backward as the oxygen stopped flowing to Grainger's brain once again. This time he didn't fight it. He just accepted it as his consciousness faded into black.

"Misery loves company, and I'm hosting a sleepover."

His eyes opened, but his vision was distorted. His neck muscles were struggling for strength as Grainger's head nodded from shoulder to shoulder. His nose was stopped up with dried blood, forcing him to breathe from his arid mouth—but at least he was breathing. He knew that he was tied up, and by the cool air and sounds of nature, he was aware that he was outside, but where? Grainger lifted his head up as his eyes adjusted to the darkness. All he could see were trees, lots of them, almost as if they surrounded him.

A silhouette came to light as it got closer, and Grainger saw his captor approaching him. Salem was wearing a black tank top now, showing off his brute build and oily, midnight skin. He squatted in front of Grainger and looked at him in an attempt to gauge if he was alert. Grainger's head was on a swivel as he tried to figure out where they were. All he could see at his feet was a feeble metal or tin flooring and a tall brick structure off in the distance. Then it hit him. He was in the middle of the woods, at the origin, the place where all of the chaos had started—they were back at the house.

"You know where you're at?" Salem whispered as if there was a chance that someone could hear them.

"The fuck are you doing, Salem? Why not just kill me when you had the chance?" Grainger questioned as he tested the durability of the rope that bound him. His knee was sore and throbbed at the cadence of his rapid heartbeat.

"Nooo," Salem smiled. "This setting is more poetic, don't you think?" He stood to his feet and spread his arms out as the thin roof creaked beneath their weight. "I'll show you where I've made my home!" He paused and dropped his arms as he looked at Grainger in disappointment. "Come on, dude. You don't know where I got that from?" He held his palms up as he welcomed a guess. "Batman, *The Dark Knight Rises*. Tell me you've seen that shit."

Grainger shook his head, not as a no to the question, but as a physical testament that he couldn't believe how Salem was taking the whole ordeal as a joke. He was quoting movies and taking extra risks just to prove what? That he was crazy and belonged in a padded room?

"You remember when how we used to play with those action figures? You always got to be Batman, and I was cool with playing Robin, but you found yourself a new little Justice League . . . forcing me to become the villain that I am. So in a sense, you made me this way. All of this is *your* fault, buddy."

"You're fucking crazy!" Grainger shouted as rage rushed through his soul.

"Go ahead and scream. Nobody will hear you, Dontarious. Nobody heard me."

Salem carefully walked to the other side of the decrepit rooftop. The rusty tin screeched beneath his boots as he apparently knew where and where not to step. Maybe he had practiced his epic ending to a book that took him years to plan. Maybe he spent countless nights out on that very roof, going over his lines and working out the bugs to his revenge.

"You want to know what pained me the most?" Salem asked from the distance.

The audience of crickets had returned, as well as a dog barking, maybe a mile away. Salem was fumbling with something as he spoke. Grainger knew that whatever he had planned would be extremely tortuous. If he simply wanted to kill him, he would've done it at the house and not taken the chance of being seen dragging him all the way out in the middle of nowhere—but then again, who would see them? Nobody but God, and Grainger was beginning to think that even the Most High had a part in this.

He struggled to free his wrists, but the rope was far too tight, and his watch had become a hindrance. Then the idea hit him.

"It wasn't the fact that you didn't stand up for me," Salem said as he walked over carrying a gas can. Dontarious twisted the watch against the leg of the chair. He now regretted wearing it so tightly as he observed Salem's actions. When he spotted the gas can in his hand, he had a feeling what Salem's plan was. He wanted to burn the house down with Grainger on top and make the perfect ending to what he viewed as a game of cat and mouse.

Salem held the can under Grainger's nostrils so he could get a strong whiff of his fate. The smell of gasoline burned his nose as he jerked his face away from the fumes.

"It was the fact that you didn't come back that hurt the most," Salem said as he stepped back. He held the can up in the air, almost at pouring angle as he paused and looked Grainger in the eyes. He wanted to see fear, but it wasn't home. Grainger wouldn't give him that much satisfaction. Plus, he needed to buy more time.

"Man, I wanted to, I really did. I just figured you were okay and didn't want to fuck with me after all of that," he confessed. It was true, and he had never admitted it out in the open till then. He wanted to go check on his friend, but the embarrassment of betrayal was too much for Grainger to face.

He had finally twisted the watch around and began to try to remove the broken glass lens. His fingertips were too big to slide beneath it, but he forced them, making a deep gash on his finger. He ignored the pain and finally removed the moon-shaped lens as he tried to mask his smile and keep a straight face. He always knew that the ugly watch would save his life one day.

"You figured I was okay?" Salem yelled in disbelief. "Y'all shot me in the leg and in the throat!"

Grainger hastily dug the glass into the ropes, cutting his wrist as well, but a few scars was a cheap price to pay for his life back. He continued cutting.

"The whole time I was in that hospital, fighting for my life, tubes in my body, voice gone, doctors saying even if I lived, I'd never speak again, nobody came to visit. Not you! Not Quinten. Not any one of your little posse showed any remorse," Salem said as he adjusted his grip on the handle. "So why should I even consider giving a fuck now?" Salem held the gas can high and began to tilt it. Dontarious almost had his hands free, but still needed more time.

"I don't know any other way to tell you that I'm sorry. I can't take it back, and believe me, if I could, I would, but that's life, Salem. Making mistakes and learning from them is life. Have you ever thought about that?"

"Lying on that bed, with this hideous scar on my neck . . . All I thought about was revenge. To make you and your friends, and your beautiful lives pay. The greatest trick the devil ever pulled was convincing the world that he didn't exist," Salem said as he began to pour the gas over the rooftop and down the massive hole from where he'd fallen fourteen years prior. He then took out a flint lighter as he looked at Grainger with a smirk. "Sometimes we create our own hell," he said as he tossed the lighter to the side, igniting the fuel. Blue flames spread over the petrol like calm tides of a beach.

It was only a matter of time before the fire made it to Grainger, so he sped up his escape plan as Salem walked over to him with his boots ablaze. "It's a shame, man. We could've been the best of friends." He turned around to walk away but was stoned by Grainger's words.

"But you forgot one thing about those cops-n-robbers games," he spat. Salem turned around and leaned in.

"And what was that?"

"The good guy always wins . . ."

The sound of the center of the roof caving in shook the night, causing Salem to glance back for a second. Grainger broke free of his restraints and slashed Salem across his face with the broken glass lens. Salem stumbled backward in pain and held his cheek as he looked at Grainger as if he'd wronged him. The fire had traveled up his pants leg and was rapidly spreading. Out of reflex he hastily patted at it to no avail.

"Here's to old friends," Grainger shouted as he picked up a two-by-four that was burning at the tip and swung it with all of his might.

Salem tried to block the strike with his forearms, but was knocked backward as he tumbled over and fell into the burning hole. He held on to the edge for his life, struggling to lift himself up, until he saw Grainger's face appear above him.

"The difference between you and me is that I'm not a killer," Grainger said as he reached his hand to save an old friend. He wanted to let him die, but his moral code kicked in. Maybe it was the fact that he was a cop, or that Salem was an old friend, but he reached down to help him.

The fire expanded and had nearly surrounded them. The frame that Salem was holding onto began to bend as he looked down at his fate. Nothing was there to catch him but more fire, a fire that he started. He looked back up and smiled at Grainger when he finally saw what he wanted to see in his eyes . . . concern.

"Salem, grab my hand, man. Stop fucking around!" Grainger said as he watched the flames close in on them.

Salem just had a goofy smile on his face. It was still a game to him. Grainger watched as Salem held on with one hand and pulled something from his back. It was a pistol, and he aimed it directly at Grainger's face with a smirk.

"We create our own hell," Salem said as he went to pull the trigger.

Grainger's survival instincts kicked in as he jumped back and rolled through the blaze. His clothes were immediately engulfed in flames, so he kept rolling until he didn't feel a surface under him. The free fall felt like an eternity, and then the ground smacked him in his back, removing all of the wind from his lungs and energy from his soul. Grainger lay there, immobilized, and watched as the house collapsed into flames.

He struggled to his knees and watched as the structure burned and began spreading to the surrounding woods. There was no way Salem survived that. Not this time.

Ding Dong Ditch

Grainger limped down the path that was now overrun with weeds and fallen branches. He could see streetlights off in the distance, peeking through the trees, so he headed in that direction. It was finally over. Salem was dead, and even though he'd rather have caught him alive to answer for his crimes, as well as clear some allegations about himself, he had to admit it felt good to finally find closure. All Grainger wanted to do now was reach civilization and call the scene in. Fire trucks would be on their way soon once neighbors noticed the flames, but Grainger also needed to call in the body that was at his house.

The body . . .

He felt odd thinking of a friend like that, but it was true. They had wasted many years, and now Quinten was gone forever. Scott was gone. Jontai was gone. Brandon was gone, but at least Salem, the root of all the evil, had met his demise.

Once the path came to an end, Grainger saw a group of bystanders on their lawns pointing at the woods. No doubt they were concerned that it could spread and potentially destroy their homes. Little did they know, there was a body in the eye of that storm, and a history of secrets that were never supposed to escape those woods.

Grainger noticed a few familiar faces; an old couple that had lived in the neighborhood for years. People were pointing at him and asking if he was okay once they saw his condition, his bloody face, his battered knee, and seared clothing, but he simply nodded and walked toward Mr. and Mrs. Barnes. Mr. Barnes recognized him and met him in the street to offer help.

"Son, is everything all right?" he asked as he put his arm around him as a crutch and led him to the curb. He placed Grainger down and looked at his wife. "Marie, call an ambulance. Son, what happened back there?" he asked. Grainger finally caught his breath and signaled at Mrs. Barnes.

"No, don't call an ambulance, I'm okay, but can I use your phone?"

She handed it to him, and he quickly dialed dispatch. He waited for a few rings, and then a familiar voice came through the receiver. "Eboni . . . it's Grainger."

"Hell to the naw! Whatever it is this time, Grainger, you can miss me with it."

"Eboni, please, this is serious. I need you send units to my house. There's a man there that's been shot and could be in critical condition or dead." Grainger waited for her response of pity for the night that he had endured. All he wanted now was for someone to act like they gave a fuck.

"Grainger, we already know about that. Units were on the scene maybe an hour ago." Grainger stood to his feet and pinned the phone closer to his ear as the sirens of the incoming fire truck grew louder.

"Is he okay? Is Quinten dead?" Grainger was afraid to hear the answer, but he needed to, for closure.

"He's stable, but in bad condition. Grainger, umm . . . Maybe you don't realize just how much shit you are truly in, so let me break it down to you, as a friend . . ."

"Eboni, listen, call Miller, and tell him to meet me at the hospital. Also send units out to the fire in Cloverdale. There's a body in an abandoned house here, that I put there. I'll explain every-thing later," Grainger said as he hung up. He handed the phone back to Mrs. Barnes, but she was looking at him weirdly after eavesdropping.

"Sir, it's official police business. I need to borrow your car," Grainger said to Mr. Barnes, who dug in his pocket and reached out to hand Grainger the keys.

When Grainger held out his hand, Mr. Barnes paused and looked him in his eyes. Grainger recognized that look. It was the same look his father used to give him.

"Whatever you did back there, son, just know that God forgives, you understand? You can still repent. You can still make it right with the Lord. You can still reach paradise in heaven as a changed man."

Grainger accepted the keys and smiled at Mr. Barnes. "Sometimes we create our own hell."

After he was held up in the lobby giving his statement and was finally released, Grainger made his way through the hospital toward Quinten's room. He had his knee evaluated and was given crutches, but his pain wasn't physical. As the crutches clanked against the white tiles, he had a bad flashback to how Neka was slain after he visited her; he had no plans of leaving his friend's side, not this time. Quinten was still unconscious, but there was an officer standing in the room on watch with another outside. Finally the precinct was taking Grainger seriously, but it was tad bit too late; Salem was dead now—Case Closed.

He watched as his friend lay there hooked up to breathing machines as he battled for his life. The doctor had informed him that Quinten's injuries were life-threatening, and that there was a strong possibility that he'd never walk again. That was painful to hear. Salem deserved the hell that he was banished to. Grainger stepped closer and just stared at Quinten. Everything could've turned out so different. Grainger could've been the one fighting for oxygen, or better yet, dead. It still hadn't clicked in his head that it was finally over, but it had to be. Enough damage had been done.

The door opened and in walked Miller. Grainger was happy to see his partner, but the look on his face didn't portray that the feeling was mutual. Miller closed the door behind him and walked over to the bedside and looked at Grainger's charred clothing.

"Grainger, they checked that scene at the abandoned house . . ."

"Okay, and? Look, I'm telling you it was self-defense. Look at me!" Grainger said as he jumped to conclusions. He was so used to his peers never believing him that his natural reaction was to defend his theory.

"Listen, there wasn't a body there . . ." Miller said as he folded his arms.

Grainger frowned his face up as he ran Miller's words back through his mental processor. "What do you mean there wasn't a body? I watched him fall into the fire myself! Tell them to search again. He *has* to be there!"

Miller placed a hand on Grainger's shoulder to calm him down. "Relax, partner . . . We believe you, and if he's out there, we will catch this guy, okay? You've been through enough tonight. Just focus on getting 100 percent tonight. We have a lot of work to do in the morning if we wanna catch this guy for real this time."

Grainger jerked his shoulder away. His anger wasn't directed at Miller himself. He was just furious that Salem might have slipped through the cracks—again. No, that was impossible. Grainger watched him die. He needed to go to the scene himself and find the body—there was no doubt about it. Salem was dead. He had to be.

Just as Grainger was about to say something a nurse walked in humming and holding a pot with a flower in it. Everyone turned toward her as she continued humming and placed the flower on a table near the window. She stood back, raised her hands to her hips, and stared at the plant.

"Kind of strange, huh?" she said as she looked at Miller and Grainger. "An aloe plant . . . but it makes sense, I guess. You know, for the healing." She winked at Miller as she started to leave, but Grainger called out to her.

"Ma'am, where did you get this?" he asked as he approached her.

"Some guy dropped it off with the receptionist in the lobby," she said as she looked at him oddly. Grainger turned and walked toward the plant. "Said he was an old friend," the nurse continued as she closed the door behind her. Miller walked over and stood beside him as Grainger flipped open the card.

Some scars never heal . . .
~The End~

Speechless

Fourteen years earlier . . .

They rolled me into a dimly lit room that somehow resembled an elevator. All of the doctors and nurses were moving so quickly, and I really didn't understand what the big deal was. It was nothing major in my book. We were just kids being kids. A simple fight that turned bad with the use of a gun. The shot in my neck pissed me off more than it hurt, so I didn't realize the severity of the wound till I finally made it home and came into the emergency room.

"Okay, we have a throat injury from a gunshot, and we suspect swelling," said the lead doctor.

I'm guessing he was in charge because he was the only person in the room who seemed to remain calm. He examined the entry wound as he leaned over my shoulder. I could smell the strong aroma of his aftershave and Diet Coke from the short distance he was standing. I wondered why all doctors were old. Could medical school really be that long?

"Salem, how are you feeling?"

I nodded my head, which really didn't answer the question, but he understood. After all, he had experienced forty years of med school so I'm sure he comprehended. I didn't know how to feel, actually. I was shot in the neck and survived, somehow . . . well, this long, at least. As long as the doctors don't kill me in surgery, I'll forever have one hell of a story to tell.

"Great. Son, we're going to have to perform surgery to make sure nothing was seriously damaged. We fear that the tissue may begin to swell, and if that happens, you will not be able to breathe. It's a simple procedure, and you will be out of here in no time. Okay?"

Once again, I nodded my head. I really didn't want to speak. At first when I got shot nothing changed, but after a while, my voice began to sound funny. It was as if I was speaking in a bathroom. My words had a weird echo and sounded distorted. I wasn't even going to go to the hospital, but once my mom got word what happened, she rushed me in the emergency room and acted out a scene from *John Q*.

"Salem, I'm going to put this mask on you. I just need you to take deep breaths and relax," the doctor said as he lifted my head up to secure the straps of the mask.

I don't know why I expected the mask to smell funny, but it didn't, and the air that circulated through was awkwardly cool. I tilted my head toward the doctor who was instructing one of the nurses to roll over a tray.

"What is this?" I asked while frowning at the way my voice sounded to me.

"It's gas," the doctor said in such a nonchalant tone.

Suddenly my panic mode kicked in. Just the sound of the word *gas* frightened me. While I was reaching for the mask, one of the nurses restrained my arm. "Just relax, Salem, you'll be asleep soon," she said in such an angelic voice.

Her eyes were a grayish blue, calming like low clouds before a brutal storm. Was having a soothing voice the criteria for becoming a nurse, so you can calm the patient while he's being put to sleep like a rabid animal? I tried to lean forward, I wanted to say something, but I couldn't. My eyelids suddenly felt heavy, like I had anvils on my lashes. As my body sank deeper into the stretcher, I wanted to yell. I even opened my mouth to scream, but I couldn't. I was speechless.

A tsunami of consciousness rolled through my body as I sat up like a child who was just baptized. The first things I noticed were all the tubes that were plugged into my body. I felt like the project of Frankenstein or a cheap entertainment system. I began to panic once again as I snatched the IV out of my arm and yanked like I was starting a lawn mower. A small puddle of blood formed and began to gain momentum as it cascaded down my arm. Glancing at my other arm, my neck felt stiff and restricted. I rubbed my throat and felt a small metal pipe inserted as I collapsed back into the cheap pillow that was provided. As I was feeling the metal tube, I also noticed a rubber tube that traced to my nostrils. I automatically thought it was a breathing tube so I snatched it.

What I thought to be half an inch turned out to be deeper. My stomach turned cartwheels, and my chest began to arch. I didn't understand what was going on, probably still in shock, so I continued to tug. The pain caused my chest to arch even higher. I relaxed and allowed my body to deflate. As I glanced down at my progress, I saw blood and chunks, which I told myself were clots of flesh. My panic meter exploded as I gripped the tube in preparation to get it over with. I waited till my heartbeat was no longer beating through my hospital gown, and then I snatched it. I felt the tube as it slid from my stomach to my nostrils, bringing along vomit and more blood.

I leaned on my side and puked out what felt to be my stomach. After the vomiting ceased, I lay there gasping for air and spitting out residue and tears that escaped my eyes and fled to my mouth. Finally when the tears stopped, along with the excess saliva, I wiped my face with the pillowcase and sat up. I was still bothered by the metal tube in my throat, but I dared not tamper with that one. I had no idea where I was going, but I knew I had to get out of that hospital. I felt lied to.

"A simple procedure, you'll be out of here in no time." The doctor lied.

As I tried to stand I felt yet another restraint, this time in my penis. My eyes turned to Volkswagen headlights as I felt the remaining tube. My only thought was that I didn't do all of that for nothing, I had to finish.

My eyes were watching God as I grasped the final tube. I didn't want to snatch this one, so I decided to just ease it out. I clawed the edge of the bed as my penis felt like it was on fire. I stopped for a second to regain my strength and motive to continue, and then went for the kill and pulled harder. What I felt next was a pain unmatched, which made the nostril tube feel like a mere Q-tip. I fell off the edge of the bed and screamed like an amateur actress in a horror movie as I knocked over the IV machine. I lay there wondering if I had actually got it out. Either way, it was pointless because I no longer had the energy to escape. This was my new reality, and I doubted I'd ever be able to escape it.

"Oh my God, Salem, what have you done?" the nurse shouted as she responded to the commotion.

She stood over me with her palms covering her mouth. At that moment I became scared. My body trembled like a Chihuahua surrounded by horny pit bulls in a wet alley. She was staring at me as if I had ripped my penis off. I reached for it to make sure it was still there, but she stopped me.

"Now we have to put everything right back in. Salem, why did you do this to yourself?" the nurse asked as she helped me back on the bed. "This is going to hurt . . ." she said with a pitiful face as she began to slide the tube back into my penis.

It hurt and stung fiercely but not as much as it did coming out.

Now, the nostril tube was a different story. As soon as she inserted the tip into my nose, my body jumped at least a foot. She put her arm across my chest to restrain me, but there was very little she could do. Another nurse rushed in to assist her in holding me down.

"Let me know if at any point you can't breathe, okay, Salem?" the first nurse asked as she continued to slide the tube through my nose and into my throat. I nodded my head violently like I was experiencing an exorcism as tears flung from my body like a bathed dog.

"Salem, can you breathe?" the second nurse asked. I wanted to answer; I needed to tell her that I couldn't. I opened my mouth, but no sound came out. I was speechless.

***

"Salem . . . Salem, can you hear me, baby?"

Minus the pain pulsating through my entire body, I felt relaxed by the nurse calling me baby. Maybe after all of the suffering I endured, I'd now be the victim of a playboy short story. With my eyes still closed I smiled at this teenage fantasy.

"Salem, baby, can you hear me, hon? This is your mother."

So much for that article, huh? My eyelids lifted slowly like ceremonial flags as I smiled at the sight of Mother. She returned the body language with a sense of relief. I tried to sit up, but she put her hand on my shoulder and instructed me to just relax. I complied, and my smile faded once I realized that the tubes were back in my body. I tried to speak, but it felt as if something was in my throat blocking my words from coming out. I couldn't even grunt or hum. My eyes translated that I was about to enter panic mode. My mother put one finger to my lips and told me to "Shhh." I was beginning to get so livid at my failed attempts that I considered biting her finger off.

"Salem, I have to tell you something. Now I want you to listen carefully and don't get crazy on me. Your vocal cords were slightly damaged so right now you can't speak . . ." She stopped and dropped her head for a second. I knew the haymaker was coming next. I didn't have time to try to guess my own fate, so I waited as she raised her head and stared me in my eyes. A pool of tears had begun to fill up her reservoir, and I knew the dam would break any moment now. "Baby, they said there is a strong possibility that you will never talk again." My dam beat hers to the punch, and she instantly tried to console me.

Never talk again? It was just a gunshot to the throat, I thought. *A weak gun at that. How did my condition come to this, to life changing?*

"Baby, don't lose hope just yet; don't give up on me, Salem. They said a *possibility,* and that could go both ways. Don't give up hope. Have faith in God and he will bring you through this. Just pray, 'cause we are all praying for you. Baby . . . It doesn't end like this."

I wasn't in the mood to hear any of that. I was just told that I would never be able to speak again. Oh, I'm sorry, there's a *possibility* . . . I knew that was just verbal medicine doctors tell the family of the victim to instill false hope.

I turned my head away from my mom and faced the wall. All I could think about was how was I going to communicate for the rest of my life. Was I going to have to moan like the elders do in rest homes requesting Jell-O? Or even worse, was I going to have to use that robotic device that chain-smokers of forty years use? My thoughts were killing me.

Trust in God . . . *God?* Could *he* give me my voice back? Would he? Of course not. What was the purpose of taking it in the first place then? To teach me a lesson? I wasn't in the mood to become some biblical puppet or a source of a frantic testimony in church. I was mad at the world, and the worst part was I couldn't tell a soul.

In the middle of my hissy fit, my silent temper tantrum at God, my mother placed a writing tablet on my shoulder. I turned my head slowly, allowing anger tears to commit suicide down my cheeks. I wanted to join them.

I glanced at the tablet, and then back at her. My face was a billboard advertising confusion. My mom handed me a pen and said, "Talk to me. Tell me how you feel. Just write it out, baby." I smirked at the fact that even in my lowest moments, my mother could still make me smile.

Our conversations through paper went on for days. I didn't remember talking to her that much when I had a voice, but we seemed to go through two tablets. Soon, I became used to this means of communication and actually pictured myself walking around with a miniature tablet to converse. I was accepting my fate. Though I didn't really understand it, I was beginning to live with it. My temporary happiness expired when my mother handed me the phone one night. My eyebrows arched to the McDonald's logo as I wondered why she would hand me the phone as if I could really reply back to whoever was there.

"Just listen for a sec. Your grandma wants to speak to you," my mom said as she assisted me in raising the phone to my ear. "Go ahead, Momma, he's listening."

"Salem? This is Grandma. I know you can't speak right now, but I just wanted you to know that I love you, and I'm praying for you; we are all praying for you. You are in everyone's thoughts and prayers. You just trust in God, and he will bring you through this. Have faith, baby. God is a mighty God and capable of anything, and he loves you dearly. We all love you dearly."

I shifted the phone to my other ear so I could hide my face from my mother. The mayor of my eyes had just received a warning that the twin dams were on the brink of collapsing once again.

"Baby, just hold on, and when times get rough, when you feel like nobody understands what you're going through, when the doctors and nurses don't seem to have a clue, talk to God. We can't hear you right now, but he can. God can hear you, Salem. Talk to him. We love you always."

The dams broke. Tears shot down my face, and I used a pillow as a silencer. The worst part about not being able to speak was not being able to tell my grandmother, "I love you too." I buried my face into the pillow to the point I almost suffocated. I wanted to say something back to Grandma—anything, just to let her know that I heard her, that I still existed. Maybe if I dialed "I Love You" through the keypad . . . 456-8396 with U as the extension. Silly thoughts flooded my brain, along with backfired tears. I wanted to say something, I needed to, but I couldn't. I opened my mouth and nothing came out. Not even the cartoon flag that read "*Bang!*" I was speechless.

I woke up in the middle of the night to the quiet but annoying hospital orchestra. IV machines dripped, heart machines beeped, in tune with breathing machines . . . well, breathing. Once my eyes were awake and adjusted to the poor lighting, I noticed just how lonely this place was. When visiting hours are over, every patient goes into the same condition—emotionally dead, and in my case, socially as well. I couldn't even talk to myself. It seemed as if my brain's secretary had lost records of what my voice sounded like. So I had a mental tablet that I wrote on just to get my thoughts out.

I focused on what my grandmother said. *"Talk to God. When nobody else can hear you, he still can."* Or something like that. I needed to fire my brain's secretary, memory, if I could ever remember to do so. I figured that since the doctors had given up on me, it wouldn't hurt to try God. At least after that, I could honestly say I exhausted all my options, and at fourteen, my life was severely changed. So I called on God. I lay there on my back with my arms crossed and stared at the ceiling. My eyes went through and focused on the stars. I connected them in a pattern that I thought was a passcode that would allow me to speak to the Almighty. I called, but there was no answer. I thought maybe I had called on the wrong name so I tried Jesus' line, and then Lord's, the Messiah's, the guy upstairs, the Creator, Bruce Almighty. Still no answer. So I left a message.

"God, if you give me my voice back, I promise you this, the whole world will hear me." I kept it short and simple. I figured he was getting a lot of calls from this hospital anyway, so I didn't take up too much of his precious time.

Once my eyes retracted back from the ceiling, I quickly glanced around the room. Surely a nurse would think I was going loony if she saw me staring at the ceiling in the middle of the night. Or maybe they see a lot of that. A smirk charged up on my face when I thought about what I just did and the crazy thoughts that I produced. It was funny to me, but I wasn't able to laugh. That action required voice. But my body wanted to. I was in dire need of a good chuckle. I felt a laugh building up in my gut and climbing to my throat. I began to choke a little, the same feeling I got when it was time to clean my trach out from the phlegm buildup. I leaned on my side and starting coughing. I tried to keep it quiet so I wouldn't alert any nurses and disturb them from reading their *Medical Science* magazines.

Wait, quiet? I was making noise! Speaking is only the controlled act of making noise. I quickly rolled back on my back and smiled. I had a change of mind so I rolled back to my side. Maybe this position was the key to the process. I built pressure up in my throat and tried to release it. I was hoping for noise, any at all, even a grunt. Nothing. I tried again. Nothing. I tried again. Nothing. Again . . . speechless. And again, till my throat felt like it would explode and my trach go flying through the ceiling.

Wait, the ceiling . . . I rolled over and concentrated. How did I used to talk? I tried to remember the simple procedure of speaking. I couldn't remember. Damn secretary. So I just lay there and tried to clear my throat. I tried over and over.

Then it happened.

Nobody truly remembers his or her first word, but I do. My first word was, "Unh," followed by a few utters of celebratory profanity. I was smiling so hard that you could probably see my wisdom teeth. So I lay there again on that pillow, which I was sure was the same pillow I lost my voice on, and I began to speak, quietly, of course. My voice sounded like heaven to me. I defied odds and did what the doctors said I wouldn't be able to do. All by myself, and, of course, God. I smiled as these thoughts became words I was actually saying out loud now. I wanted to tell someone, but whom? So I waited. Visiting hours would start in a couple of hours.

I stayed in the same position for hours that felt like days trying my best to suppress my smile as my mother entered the room. "Good morning, baby," she said as she rubbed my forehead with both sides of her hands. I guess even in hospitals mothers will still play doctor.

"How are you feeling today, better?" she asked as she reached for the tablet on the nightstand.

She handed it to me, along with the pen, and waited on my reply. I held the tablet in front of my face to hide my wisdom teeth as I pretended to write an answer. Then I handed her back the blank tablet. She glanced at it, and then back at me with a puzzled look. I charged my throat up and fired.

"I'm doing fine, Mama. How are you?" I said with the biggest smile my facial muscles would allow.

Her hands shot to her mouth as she dropped the tablet. She began to stumble backward and collapsed in the visitor's chair with her hands still covering her trembling lips. I sat up to see if she was okay. I feared that I had possibly given her a heart attack. But she just stared at me with watery eyes soaking through her fingertips.

"Momma, are you okay?" I asked in my most worried voice. She didn't reply. She just stared at me, crying. She was speechless.

OTHER TITLES BY NILES MANNING